Neither one wanted the evening to end.

Curley kept a protective arm over her shoulder. "You know," he said, "you're a courageous woman, and I admire that."

"Me? I'm merely working for what I feel is right."

"Not all women would go to such lengths to try to make sense of this crazy world. You're like a missionary."

They stopped at her cabin door. "My mission is to find the truth and reveal it to the world, so people can form their own opinions."

"Well said! If you ever run for president, I'll vote for you."

She loved the amusement that flickered in his eyes and the companionship they shared. As she watched, the amusement began to disappear and a contemplative look came into his hazel eyes.

She thought for a moment he was going to kiss her, but he said, "Be careful, Princess. Don't trust everything you see in Germany to be as it seems."

"But that's why I'm going!" she said with a smile.

He lifted his brows in acceptance, and said, "Just remember. Be careful."

JANE LAMUNYON says she wrote her first inspirational romance because "I want to show that a fulfilling romantic relationship takes three persons: a man, a woman, and God." Jane is a wife, mother, and grandmother who lives in Southern California.

Books by Jane LaMunyon

HEARTSONG PRESENTS
HP156—Fly Away Home

Escape
on the Wind

Jane LaMunyon

Heartsong Presents

This book is dedicated to my husband Jim, an aviation expert, who never tired of answering my many questions about planes and flying techniques. It is also dedicated to three of my relatives whose names I found in Jerusalem's Yad Vashem's records of those taken to Nazi concentration camps: Elias van der Noot, 8-4-17 to 8-27-43, Auschwitz; Hans Jack van der Noot, 9-28-42 to 8-27-43, Auschwitz; and Louis van der Noot, 5-16-10 to 3-26-43, Sobibor.

A note from the Author:
I love to hear from my readers! You may write to me at the following address: **Jane LaMunyon**
Author Relations
P.O. Box 719
Uhrichsville, OH 44683

ISBN 1-57748-248-4

ESCAPE ON THE WIND

Cover illustration by John Monteleone.

one

September 2, 1934

After Amanda's birthday dinner, Stanley, the servant, cleared away the crystal water goblets, then pushed a linen-covered cart to the table, between Amanda and her father. Stanley removed the white linen to reveal a pile of brightly wrapped presents, then moved back to stand beside the door.

"Thank you, Stanley," said Amanda's mother. Her blue eyes sparkled in her round face as she cast a satisfied look at the dinner guests. The double circle of braids crowning her head glowed softly in the light from the chandelier.

With a dimpled grin, Amanda's sister Victoria said, "Open them! I can't bear the waiting!" Her two aunts nodded fondly in agreement.

Amanda opened her presents, thanking her family for the lovely items, some of which were clearly meant for her hope chest. The French linen tablecloth with Battenburg lace edging from Aunt Edith brought admiring sighs from the guests, but Amanda wondered if she'd ever have a use for it as she quietly folded it back into its box. Aunt Emma's gift was a dozen matching napkins.

Her father presented her with a leather-bound first edition of Stendhal's works. She gasped in pleasure, running her hands over the gilt letters of the top book *Lucien Leuven.* "Oh, Father, you remembered. Thank you!"

Her father nodded brusquely. "Hm. Yes. You always did favor those French writers."

Soon there was a pile of wrapping paper on the floor beside her chair, the boxes stacked neatly on the tray. "Thank you, all," said Amanda. "I am—"

"Wait!" Delbert pushed his chair back and stood. He flashed

5

a smile at the seated guests, then took Amanda's hand, drawing her to her feet. "I haven't presented my gift yet."

Amanda looked at him with some confusion. She glanced at her father, leaning back in his chair, looking smugly satisfied; and then her mother, who clasped her hands with anticipation.

"Amanda, we've grown up together," Delbert began. "Everyone here knows how I feel about you."

Amanda could feel her face coloring.

Delbert's brilliant dark eyes glittered as he continued. "On this auspicious occasion, and before these beloved guests, I offer this, a token of my love and esteem." He pulled a small box from his jacket pocket and presented it to her.

She almost recoiled from it, a premonition shouting warnings in her head, but she held out her hand and he laid the box in her palm. *Let it be a locket,* she prayed silently as she slowly lifted the lid.

But it wasn't. A large marquise diamond, flanked by two smaller ones in a graceful setting, winked up at her. She stared at it in shock.

"Will you marry me, Amanda Chase? Say yes, and make me the happiest man in the world."

Taking a deep breath, her cheeks burning, she looked away. Her father didn't seemed surprised. The image of him and Delbert in deep discussion last week filled her mind. Now her family eagerly watched for her reply.

Delbert flashed a bright, confident smile.

She pushed back a flush of anger with a small laugh. Her Aunt Emma smiled and wiped her eyes with a lace handkerchief. With iron control, Amanda said, "I'm speechless! Delbert, this is such a surprise; I don't know what to say."

She could almost hear the silent group saying, *Say yes, say yes.*

She closed the lid over the sparkling diamond. "I'm too overwhelmed to answer right now." She set the box on the table. "Thank you all, and please excuse me." With her head held high, she walked out of the room.

Her heels clicked on the parquet floor of the hallway as she fled. Mrs. Heathman, the cook, pushed the swinging kitchen door open. "Happy birthday, Miss!" she said.

Amanda glanced back, a tight smile hurting her face. "Thank you." Continuing on through the parlor, she made a quick decision not to go upstairs to her room and went out the front door.

The cool night air did little to dampen her hot anger. She stomped her way past the two cars parked out front, through the posts lighting the driveway, over the grass to the knoll. She took a few deep breaths to calm herself. Holding onto a low branch, she looked out over the lights of Boston below.

How could Delbert humiliate her? Sure, they'd been friends for the last two years, but that's all it was—friendship. They'd talked about marriage and she'd explained that marriage and family weren't in her plans right now. He contended that *settling down* was what a woman must do—take care of home, family, and her man.

That's fine for Mother, Amanda thought. *But not for me. Not yet.* She sighed with regret, thinking of her mother's and aunts' looks of bright anticipation. To them there was no higher call than that of wife and mother. *But there must be something more,* thought Amanda. Some warm, even passionate feelings. And there should be spiritual agreement. Delbert always shrugged when she brought up God, as though the topic wasn't important to him.

As she tiptoed through the wet grass to the stone bench, she heard the front door close and Delbert calling her. She glanced back to see him walking down the driveway behind the post-lights. She felt her indignation rise in response to his approach.

It's time to take care of this, she thought. "I'm here!" she called.

Peering through the darkness, he loped across the grass toward her.

Knees pushed into the stone bench, hands gripping its back, she watched him approach. His long legs took the distance quickly. He looked perfect in his three-piece suit and tie, his dark hair neatly combed back.

"Sweet girl, are you all right?" He came around the bench to her side. She looked away.

"What?" he asked, his eyes clouding with concern.

"I'm fine, Delbert." She sat and slipped off her shoes, setting them beside her. He sat too, the shoes between them.

He reached into his pocket and brought out the ring box again. "I may have made a mistake, darling. Maybe you'd rather I asked you privately to marry me."

Leaning forward, he presented the box again. Putting his right arm along the bench back he stroked her neck slowly. "Will you, Amanda? You know how much I care for you."

She stared into the bright luster of his eyes. "Delbert, you and I are too different to ever become one." She folded her hands in her lap, ignoring the box.

"I know your job is important to you, but my company is doing well, and I make more than enough money to support us." He continued to hold the box toward her. "You can go to church, but you'll be so busy with other things, you won't have time for much else."

"It's not going to church or my job, Delbert." She paused for a second, then asked, "What 'other things' would keep me busy?"

"Oh, the running of our home, our social engagements, and—you know—being my wife."

"You're asking me to give up everything to take on the job of making your life easy?"

"It's a big responsibility," he said.

"And what I do now isn't?"

He looked baffled. "Sure it is. I'm proud of your little newspaper stories. But someday you'll have to stop examining other people's lives and settle down to a real life of your own, you know—your own home and family."

She froze, her words coming out in icy chips. "I have a real life. And my work is more than 'little newspaper stories about other people's lives.' "

He lowered the box, resting it in his lap. "You want that

more than a loving husband and home of your own?"

"Delbert, you're a good person, and you're doing well in your profession. But I don't feel any more for you than I would a good friend. I do know that I couldn't love anyone enough to give up my beliefs and my life's work."

An expression of pained tolerance swept over his face. "I'll go to church with you, Sweetheart."

She expelled her breath in aggravated surprise. "You don't understand! Going to church isn't the same thing as being a Christian."

With a confused expression, he stared at her. "What do you mean?"

"I mean, it's more than walking in the church door, more than just *saying* you're a Christian. It's a whole new life, it's being born again."

"You're talking in riddles, my dear."

"No. I've told you before, and you've heard it when you went to church with me. It's believing that Jesus is the Son of God, that He was born of a virgin and died on the cross for your sin, that He ascended to heaven and sits at God's side. It means that you look for Him to come again as He said He would."

"Well, that's a lot to think about." He thrust the ring box back toward her. "Keep this, and think about our engagement."

She jumped up and slipped her shoes on. "We've never really communicated, have we, Delbert?" She walked away. There was nothing more to say.

He followed her back into the house. Her aunt, uncle, and two cousins were leaving. "Here are the lovebirds!" said Aunt Joan, reaching for her left hand. "Let me see the ring!"

Amanda pulled her hand back. "I'm not wearing it."

"Yet." Uncle Mark put his arm around her shoulder and winked at her. "He's a prize, girl. Don't let him get away."

Amanda slipped her arm around her uncle's waist and held out her hand to her aunt. "Thanks for coming, all of you."

After all the guests had gone home, Amanda's father took her arm and said, "Come with me. I want to talk to you." He led her to the study. Victoria followed them, eyes wide and curious.

"Maybe Victoria should go on up to her room now," said her mother, with an appeal in her glance to her husband.

"No. Victoria is part of the family, and she'll learn something."

Still strong with the resolve to hang onto her career, and the feeling that she'd been right to refuse Delbert's proposal, Amanda closed the study door and turned to face her father.

She'd always liked this room, with its wall of books, the smell of leather, and the solidarity of the huge mahogany desk where her father worked with his gallery accounts. He stood beside it now, resting one hand on the edge. Her mother sat with her back erect in the leather chair beside the fireplace and folded her hands in her lap, waiting. Victoria leaned against the bookshelf, her slim legs crossed.

Her father stared at Amanda beneath heavy eyebrows. "I'm not going to beat around the bush with small talk. Tonight we celebrated your twenty-fourth birthday, and I want to know why you didn't accept the proposal from that decent young man."

Before Amanda could answer, her mother spoke, her words coming rapidly as if she could no longer hold them back. "I can't imagine what you're thinking! You're twenty-four years old! Twenty-four! And you're still a spinster. When I was your age, I'd been married for five years and had a child. Delbert's a good man, with a successful business, which as you know, in these times is a miracle. I know you like him. How could you turn him down? And in front of everyone!"

Amanda carefully took a deep breath to stay calm.

Victoria chuckled. "Spinster?" She wrapped a blond curl around her fingers, smiling at the odd idea.

"What your mother is trying to say," her father said, "is that we gave you the best education money could buy—how many girls study at the Sorbonne in Paris these days? You've traveled the world, had all the right social connections, and for what? Here you are, still single at an age when most young women are taking care of their own households and husbands."

Her mother nodded her head. "You don't visit your friends lately. They *are* married, and you don't have much in common with them anymore."

"My career. . ."

"Your what?" Her father glared at her. "Is that why you're so often late for dinner? Were you out making headlines for that rag? Were you scooping Walter Winchell on the Boston Ladies' Sewing Guild luncheon? You call that a career?"

Amanda answered with quiet firmness. "The *Boston Chronicle* isn't a 'rag.' It's a reputable newspaper."

Victoria's hands flew to her mouth to cover a smile, and Amanda hastily added, "Beating Walter Winchell to a story has never been my goal." Today she had covered the South Boston Women's Croquet tournament. That morning in the seedy part of town she took notes and talked to people for a feature story on the plight of the depression's abandoned children. But she wouldn't give her father the satisfaction of either laughing at her trivial croquet story, or berating her for the danger of consorting with 'undesirables.'

"All right. So you don't want to be a better reporter than Winchell. That puts us back to my original question. Just what *do* you plan to do with your life?"

Her mother leaned forward in the chair, her blue eyes pleading with Amanda to agree with her. "Her goal is the same as any normal young woman. A home and family—eventually. Am I right?" To punctuate her point, she added, "After all, you're not getting any younger."

Amanda gazed down at the familiar scrolled pattern on the Turkish rug and girded her resolve. She looked up at them. "Mother, Dad, I've always done my best in what you've asked me to do. I went through school earning honors, and I was valedictorian at college graduation. Should all that knowledge go to waste while I plan menus and entertain the hoi polloi for the benefit of some man?" She cast an affectionate look to her mother. "You're a wonderful wife and mother, but I'm not you. I'm just starting my career, and it's important to me. I'm sorry if I'm a disappointment to you, but I can't give up my life to some man and never know what I could have done or been."

She looked her father right in his eyes and struggled to keep from trembling. "I must devote my life to improving this world in the best way I know how, by documenting and exposing society's goodness and evils. If I can make someone understand this world a little better and change a life because of it, then I will have been successful. That's my goal."

"Poppycock! Most people glance over headlines, find the comics and crossword puzzles, then wrap their garbage in the papers. The poor wretches sleeping on park benches cover themselves with it, and I hear that they even slip them inside their shoes to cover the holes. We're in a depression right now, and I don't know how that rag stays in business."

Amanda bit her lips together. This was as frustrating as the scene she'd had with Delbert. She hadn't communicated the inner flame, her passion for her career. They didn't understand.

"What you're going to do is wake up and do what's right. I won't support this hobby you're glorifying into a career. You resign and either marry Delbert or start seeing other men, with the intention of being a real woman and settling down."

Stunned, she stared at him. "I am a real woman, Father!"

His gaze never wavered. "We'll do all we can to help you. But if you don't take your responsibilities seriously, I'll be forced to take steps to persuade you to comply."

Her mother leaned forward, her elbows resting on the chair arm. Her face lighted up with joy. "Think about it, Amanda. We can have a gala engagement affair; we'll invite everyone who is anyone, it'll be the event of the season, and—"

"Oh, I do so adore parties," said Victoria, looking into a scene only she could see. "I can see the Chase sisters turn this town on its ear!" She frowned as Amanda moved her head slightly from side to side. "Oh, don't be so dreary. It'd be such fun."

Amanda kept her eyes locked with her father's. "What steps?"

"Face it, girl. Your job is taking you nowhere. If you persist you'll never find a man to take care of you and you'll grow old, living at home. That would be detrimental to you, and an embarrassment to us. I'd be a poor father to allow that to happen. There is no option. You must give up this notion of saving the world, and face reality."

"Or?" Amanda's voice was so low, she wasn't sure her father heard her.

"Or I'll have to curtail your allowance, and speak to your editor and resign for you. Then you'll take the proper responsibilities of a young woman."

She tried to read regret or hesitation in his eyes, but she could detect neither. His gaze hid any emotions he might be feeling.

She was no longer a child he could order to take a certain class in school or dictate who she could and couldn't visit. But she knew him well enough to know that approaching her editor was no idle threat. Cold fear clenched her stomach, but she resisted it with every ounce of energy she could muster, lifted her chin, and said, "I've planned my career, my life. I told Delbert I can't give up my plans for him, or anybody." She broke her gaze with her father to look at her mother, who was staring at her with stunned disbelief. "I'm sorry," she said to both of them.

"I know this is hard for you to understand," said her father, "but I am doing what's best for you. I'll give you a week before I take action. Do you understand?" She nodded. "Good. You're a smart girl. I fully expect by next week you'll be back on course toward a full and happy life."

❧

Later, she paced restlessly in her room. Although her father still didn't believe her, for the first time in her life she had defied him. It was scary, but she had to do it. She planned on being independent eventually, before the shadowy idea of marriage and family became a reality. In these modern times lots of women had careers. She mentally tallied up her material assets: her savings account, her annuity, which she'd received from Grandpa Morganstern when she turned twenty-one, and her meager pay from the *Chronicle.*

She pushed the balcony window open and stepped out into the cool night air. Hugging her shoulders, she looked up. "Oh, God, what am I going to do? I feel a restless urge toward something; I don't know what." A breeze trembled through the oak tree, and after another minute she went back inside. They thought she couldn't take care of herself? Well, she vowed to prove them wrong.

two

Curley Cameron's eyes snapped open. The rain had quit. A drop of water snaked down the closed window as the pre-dawn light glowed feebly into the barracks room. Curley pushed off the heavy cover, shivering as he crossed the room to the window. He slid it up, and leaned out into the coolness with his hands braced on the sill.

Wildflowers bloomed nearby, and their fragrance sur-rounded him. The clouds were mostly gone, the wind was light, and he knew if he got high enough he could see for miles. "Hot dog!" he said to the new day, and quickly dressed.

He stuffed his few belongings into his duffel bag, and took a last look around before quietly closing the door behind him and tiptoeing past closed doors; most of the airmen were still asleep. In the latrine, he splashed icy water on his face, shaved quickly, and left for the mess hall and a cup of coffee.

He saluted to the officer of the day, who was also up early for his duties. Avoiding puddles of leftover rain, he scanned the horizon over the airstrip, and with long happy strides, walked faster. Flying weather at last! The reveille bugle pierced the air as he went inside the warm mess hall. Chow wasn't ready, but the cook gave him toast and jam with his coffee.

Back outside, he slipped the catch from the hangar door and pushed it sideways. It was still dark inside, but dawn light glowing behind him touched the propeller with a gentle gleam. "Hello, Sweetheart," he said, patting his DeHaviland Moth. "We're going up today!" A Harley-Davidson crunched through the gravel toward him, its lights still on, as he pushed all the hangar doors to the side, opening it up.

He circled the plane, checking for loose bolts, feeling for

15

uneven wing surfaces, and anything else that could cause an in-flight problem. When he finished the sky was fully light, and he could hear guys moving around on the other side of the wall. He stuck his head outside, to see two men pushing a P-26A out of a hangar down the line.

By 6:30 A.M. the hangar doors were all open but one, four planes had already taken off, and Curley had gotten assistance in pulling his Moth out onto the tarmac. He stowed his duffel bag in the back, and fueled up, then pulled his clipboard out from under his seat and stood beside the struts, studying it.

He'd mapped out his route to California three days ago, before the rains slowed him down, and he had studied it every day, marking airfields he'd touch down in. Nevertheless, he checked the flight plan once more, memorizing the route.

His concentration was interrupted by the warmth of a soft body pressed to his back and smooth white arms circling his chest.

He lowered the clipboard to his side and turned. She held on so tightly, he had to lift his left arm over her head. He grinned down at her. "Ah, Jenny! What brings you out so early?"

Her lips puckered into a lovely pout. "I think you're leaving without saying good-bye."

"Honey, you know I have business to take care of."

Her chocolate-colored eyes gazed at him wistfully. Then she stood on tiptoe and put her head on his shoulder and nuzzled his neck. "Stay one more day," she murmured.

He stepped back and took her face in his large hand. "It's time. I have to go."

Her eyes narrowed with sudden anger. "You think you can just toss me aside like an old shop rag?" She looked down her nose at him under half-closed eyes. "I have others fellas calling on me, you know."

"I know that, Sweet One. You're much too fine a girl for the likes of me." He rubbed her chin gently with his thumb.

She stared over his shoulder at the airplane. Not meeting his eyes, she said, almost to herself, "You won't be back." She turned her compelling eyes on him, and he had to force himself to pull his hand away from her soft cheek and step back.

He shook his head slowly. "Don't think about it. Turn around, walk away, and forget about me."

"But we. . .I. . ." She looked around in desperation as if searching for the answer to a confusing puzzle. "You can't just leave!"

He shook his head. "I go where the Army Air Corps sends me. That's the fact of it."

"But—"

He put his finger on her lips, not wanting to prolong their good-byes. Holding the clipboard at his chest between them, he gave her a light kiss on her cheek and said, "Good-bye, Jenny."

She stared at him for a moment, then raised her chin and defiantly informed him, "In two weeks—in two minutes, I'll have forgotten you, like this!" She snapped her fingers and walked away without a backward glance.

Curley watched her walk away, feeling admiration for the way she turned the situation around to seem as if she were leaving him instead. *Women!* he thought. They craved rose-covered cottages and forever-afters. He never met one who didn't either hint, or downright talk openly about it. Why were they always in such a hurry to get themselves tied down?

He glanced at his flight map, then walked back to the hangar, thinking of how dependent women were, needing a man to complete their lives. *Bless them, though, they sure make life a lot more interesting,* he thought, smiling.

His thoughts were interrupted by a summons to the base commander's office.

He entered the colonel's office, saluted and said, "Reporting as ordered, sir." He stood at attention until the commanding officer said, "At ease, Captain." The colonel tapped the papers on his desk with his pencil. "Captain Cameron, I have orders here that you are to depart immediately and report to General Franklin in Washington."

"Sir?" Curley eyed the official envelope under the colonel's fingers. "I'm geared up and ready to report to Muroc Air Base."

The colonel handed him the sealed orders. "Report to the general at eleven-hundred hours."

"Yes, sir." Curley took the envelope, saluted, and left the CO's office, wondering what this was all about. He'd been looking forward to going back to California where the only family he knew waited for him.

He pushed his plane back into the hangar. Approaching the CB-5 he'd fly to D.C., the mechanics and pilots he'd worked with wished him well.

The minute the wheels left the runway, as always he felt as though a weight holding him to the ground snapped free, leaving him to float on the air, climb the currents, and ride the sky. This was where he belonged. Everything below seemed unreal. This was reality. He soared into the heavens, his plane merely an extension of himself, and then dipped the left wing, heading in a northerly direction toward Washington, D.C.

❧

Amanda drove herself to work Monday morning, with Delbert following. He'd come by to pick her up, but keeping her goal in mind, she had insisted on driving herself.

Her father's threat worried her. Would Mr. Mitchell fire her at her father's request? He certainly wouldn't want trouble from one of the most prestigious families in Boston. And her stories hadn't exactly been banner headlines. But she didn't get the plum assignments either, and there was only so much she could do with the topics she covered.

Her hands gripped the steering wheel as she drove through neighborhoods that had once housed families filled with dreams and hopes. With the Great Depression they faced the terrible loss of work, and few managed to keep their homes. Grass and weeds stood tall in the small yards in front of the row of forlorn-looking houses. Downtown the employment office was besieged by a crowd, waiting for the doors to open. For every rare job offer, a hundred hungry people applied. She didn't notice until she arrived at the *Chronicle* building that Delbert was no longer following her.

Inside, the smell of paper, ink, and pencils settled over her like a familiar cloak. Noise filled the room: the clatter of typewriters, ringing phones, and the hum of the fan which didn't efficiently rid the room of cigarette smoke. Her coworkers glanced up from their work and smiled as she passed.

She stood over her desk, checking for messages. She was relieved to see a note from Mr. Mitchell, asking her to come to his office as soon as she arrived. She wanted to see him right away, too.

She tucked her croquet tournament and abandoned children's stories under her arm and made her way through the desks to the glassed-in corner office. Behind his desk, Titus Mitchell leaned forward, clutching the telephone in one hand. With the phone's earpiece in his other hand, he gestured her to come inside.

She paused inside the door, but he motioned her to sit, and she perched on the edge of the chair, her stories on her lap. Mitchell paced behind his desk with restless energy, the phone stand in one hand and the ear piece in the other. In his dynamic presence, Amanda felt her resolve shrinking.

He finally hung up the phone and smiled at her. Glancing at the papers in her lap, he said, "Croquet story?"

"Yes. And a feature on the plight of homeless waifs."

He grimaced. "Too depressing. I don't—"

"There's a group of people trying to help. This is an upbeat story, with hope."

"Well, lemme see it, and I'll let you know." He held out his hand, and she placed her stories in it. He'd barely glanced at the top page when Eileen, his secretary, opened the door.

"The battle between hired goons filling strikers' jobs in Pittsburgh is getting bloody. Details are starting to come through on the ticker tape," she said.

"I'll be right out." He looked at Amanda and said, "I want you to interview Edith Barnett about the Women's Works Program."

"Yes, sir."

"And see what you can find out about the Boston Relief Committee's plan to distribute food to the poor."

"We did a story on BRC last week."

He shrugged. "Then find a new angle."

"Mr. Mitchell, I. . ." Amanda's fingers tensed in her lap, and she chided herself for tending to stammer.

Mitchell, now standing at the door, glanced at the activity in the newsroom, then turned his gray eyes on her. "Yes?"

She sat straighter in her chair, gathering her courage. "I'd like to do a big story. Something that will be different from anything the *Chronicle* has ever done."

"And I assume you have that big story figured out?"

"As a matter of fact, yes," she said. "Many papers, even ours, have run stories about Germany's prosperity and growth since they elected Adolf Hitler. Clean streets, happy people, all with jobs, and order from the chaos they used to have."

"Yes, so? That's not news."

She leaned forward. "It's not true." She saw that he was going to argue, so she quickly added, "Not all of it."

He hardened his mouth around the word, "Propaganda?" He stepped closer to her. "We don't print propaganda!"

"No, of course not," she agreed. "I think we just don't have the complete story."

"And you, I suppose, can get this complete story?" He looked at her as one would at a child who'd just said she'd had breakfast with President Roosevelt.

With quiet but firm resolution, she said, "My mother's sister and family live in a small town near Berlin. They're Jewish, and from their letters I know it's not all peaches and cream there. I intend to bring back the real story."

"Girlie, you're good at what you do. Stick to fashion and society news. If there are sinister happenings in Germany, it'll get back to us. Besides, if what you say is true, it could be risky."

"I know there's a story there, and I can cover it, because I have sources the correspondents there don't have. I'll write a story that will touch our readers' hearts."

He craned his neck to see if the Teletype story had started coming. "No Germany trip. You don't even have an expense account. You think I'd send you on a wild goose chase halfway across the world?" He turned and shook his head in disbelief.

"I'll cover the expenses myself, and when I bring you my story, I want a byline, and better assignments."

He laughed. "Amanda, girl, you just want a vacation." She stood as a crowd gathered around the ticker-tape machine. He left to get the tape as it came ticking out and didn't look back at her.

Amanda stomped back to her desk. He'd laughed at her! This was the last straw. She found a paper sack in the supply closet and began dumping her personal belongings from her desk. After several phone attempts, she found a boat going to Europe in two days. She'd have to share a cabin, but that was fine with her. She typed a letter to her Aunt Esther to tell her she was coming and a note to Mr. Mitchell.

She went home to pack, vowing to bring back a story that would knock the socks off Mr. Titus Mitchell, make people think, and earn her a headline and a place on his reporting staff. There were respected women journalists in this world. It was time for the *Boston Chronicle* to enter the twentieth century.

As she drove up the curving driveway at home, she braced herself for the scene that would follow when she told her mother and father of her plans.

⁂

Curley touched down at the airfield near Washington, at 10:15 A.M. and taxied to a parking area as directed by the ground crew. He shut down the engine, grabbed his duffel bag, and climbed out onto the tarmac. The flight-line sergeant asked, "Any problems with this ship we need to look after?"

"No. No problems. She's a good little plane."

A soldier drove up in a pickup truck, leaped out, and saluted. Curley tossed his duffel bag in the back and they drove to the flight operations building where Curley logged in, then to the headquarters building.

In the latrine, he took off his flight suit, put on his uniform, and combed his hair. A quick look in the mirror told him he was presentable.

In the general's anteroom he waited on a stiff wooden chair. Finally, the secretary announced that General Franklin would see him. Curley took a deep breath and marched into the general's office. He saluted and said, "James Lee Cameron reporting as ordered, sir."

In his early forties, General Franklin's close-cropped hair had a touch of gray at the temples, and a thick mustache covered his upper lip. Curley stood, legs spaced apart, hands behind his back, watching the general scrutinize him with the eye of a man sizing up a new team player. "Captain," he said, "drag up a chair and make yourself comfortable. How about a cup of coffee?"

"Thank you, sir."

General Franklin touched a button and before Curley got the chair pulled toward the large desk, his secretary rushed in, then out again to fetch the coffee.

The general settled back in his chair. "Captain, I have a mission that requires a special man. You're one of our best pilots, you know as much about the planes as the mechanics, and you've shown yourself to be, shall we say, adventuresome. I've followed your career and feel you're the man for the job. Are you interested? Before you answer, you should know that if you decline it won't be held against you."

Curley took a quick breath, curious about the assignment, then answered, "Yes, sir. I'm interested."

"Good. Now here's the plan: Our English friends tell us the Germans are starting to rearm in violation of the Treaty of Versailles, and are building their air force back up." The general leaned forward and said, "I've made arrangements with the RAF. Your mission, in an unofficial capacity, will be to travel into Germany and find out what you can. Bring back facts and figures. Report to no one but me when you return.

"While in England you will study German terrain and politics. Also, an instructor will teach you phrases and as much

German language as you can absorb in ten days. Your unofficial duties will be as a civilian delivering a Vega to Holland. You've been checked out on the 247. It's been equipped with extra gas tanks, and fuel diverters. You'll be on the crew taking it to England tomorrow afternoon. Any questions?"

Besides the thrill of flying the big new 247, Curley had lots of questions. For one thing, he knew that a military man out of uniform and in civilian clothes sent into another country can be shot as a spy. But then, Germany was not an enemy. He asked, "What's my time period for this surveillance?"

"Take as long as you need, within reason. I expect you to use some of that ingenuity you displayed while you were a cadet."

By the glint of amusement in the general's eyes, Curley knew he meant the weekend air shows he participated in every chance he got. He nodded. "Yes, sir."

That afternoon he visited the Post Exchange and bought slacks, a shirt, a jacket, and a suitcase to put them in. The next afternoon he stowed his duffel bag full of military clothes in the base locker. Wearing his flight suit, he carried his new suitcase filled with civilian clothes onto the big 247.

three

Perched on the edge of her bed, Amanda frowned over her open suitcase, stuffed with so many clothes the lid wouldn't close. Victoria sat cross-legged, resting her back against the headboard, her white batiste nightgown stretched over her knees. The turmoil that had followed Amanda's announcement of her trip to Germany hadn't fazed Victoria; she was elated over Amanda's adventure.

Amanda, however, swallowed hard, bravely choosing clothes for the trip, while her heart was in chaos. She grieved at the rift between her and her father, but she felt a strong need to prove she was a person in her own right.

Victoria picked up a peach-colored sweater from a pile beside the suitcase. "I can see you strolling the deck, looking out over the ocean. A handsome man comes up." She caressed the soft wool with a faraway, dreamy look. "You shiver slightly, he whips off his jacket, and puts it across your shoulders. You. . ."

Amanda rolled her eyes. "There's a full moon, a zillion stars, and the man looks like Clark Gable. Which movie did you see that in?"

Victoria dropped the sweater on the bed "No, silly, it's Delbert! He's as handsome as Gable!" She leaned forward and looked into Amanda's face. "Just think of it—this could be your honeymoon trip!" She sat back, grinning.

Amanda solemnly studied the clothes stacked in the suitcase. She slipped her hand between two skirts and carefully pulled one out. "The only men paying any attention to me will be the porter carrying these suitcases and the dining room waiter," she said, balancing the skirt on the discard pile.

Victoria expelled a long sigh and clasped her hands behind her head, lifting her hair. Blond curls bounced beside her sparkling eyes. "Delbert can put his arm around me anytime!"

"Victoria!"

"What? I'm sixteen, and I've been kissed. Lots of times."

Amanda paused with her hand on the suitcase. "Oh? When?"

Victoria looked at the ceiling and pursed her lips, as if trying to remember all of them. Amanda eyed her suspiciously, as the door opened and their mother came in, a worried expression chiseling a vertical line between her eyebrows.

Amanda's throat tightened at her mother's pained expression. Holding in her churning emotions, she turned and shut the suitcase with a click of finality.

"Amanda," her mother began, "Please. . ."

"Mom, it's all right." Leaning over the closed suitcase, she bit her upper lip to keep control. If she explained once more would her mother understand? She touched her mother's shoulder and said, "Please believe me, Mom. This is something I have to do."

Her mother's eyes misted over. "But it's so sudden, and your father. . ."

"I know," Amanda said softly, "Dad doesn't understand; but I'll be fine. Really. I'll be with Aunt Esther and Uncle Jacob, and I'll write as soon as the ship docks in London."

Her mother still looked worried, but Amanda knew that she was looking forward to hearing firsthand news of her family.

Although her mother had left the Jewish faith when she married Amanda's father, the ties between the two families had remained strong down through the years, and they had visited back and forth, the children spending summers together with one family or another. In fact, it was during one of those summers that Amanda's nanny, Miss Whitney, had taken Amanda and her cousin Martha with her to church, and both girls had accepted Christ as their Savior. Amanda smiled, remembering, and the tiny lines that puckered her mother's forehead disappeared. "Well," her mother said, "so long as you're with your aunt and uncle, I suppose you'll be all right."

&

The next morning Amanda, her mother, and sister rode to the

pier in a taxi. Her father, unwilling to condone any part of her crazy notion, had said his good-byes at the front door. He'd given Amanda a stiff hug, and slipped two fifty-dollar bills into her hand.

On board the ship, Victoria eyed each of the passengers, looking for celebrities; and quite a few male heads turned toward her youthful attractiveness.

At Amanda's cabin, they found suitcases on one bed, and a cosmetic bag open with a turquoise scarf lying beside it on the dresser. Her mother agreed the cabin was "nice," but insisted that Amanda should have it to herself. "And you didn't bring enough clothes," she added.

"Mother, I have to carry both suitcases. What would I do with a trunk?"

"There are ways. Porters are everywhere."

Amanda put her arm across her mother's shoulders. "Look at it this way. At least Uncle Jacob won't think I'm moving in."

Her mother's eyes grew teary. Amanda hugged her and said, "I'll be all right, Mom. Really."

"I hope so," her mother said, dabbing at her eyes as she looked at Amanda sadly.

Victoria took Amanda's hand. "It's not too late for me to come along." Before Amanda could say anything, she continued, "I know I don't have clothes, but we could go shopping in London. Wouldn't that be a lark?"

Her mother smiled weakly and took Victoria's hand. "You're coming home with me. I'm not letting both my girls go away at once."

Amanda walked them to the ramp, and they said their last good-byes. A few minutes later the ship moved away from the shore. She'd been on many departing ships, but this time it seemed as though the ship sliding away from the shore was like fate, pulling her away from her family toward a new destiny. The shouts of the crowd faded away as they receded with the harbor, until her mother and sister were no longer distinguishable.

Swept along in the swarm of exhilarated passengers leaving

the rail, she left them at the hallway to her cabin, while they headed for a party in the ballroom. The hallway was deserted except for a young mother holding the hand of a toddling little boy. They nodded and Amanda continued on.

Inside her cabin, the feeling of unreality was underscored by the ship's gentle swaying. Amanda sat on her bed, absorbing the almost monastic solitude. After a moment she reached inside her carryall bag for her notebook and pen. She'd really done it; she had asserted her independence, and was bound for Germany.

She slowly rotated the top of the pen between her teeth, lost in thought. Her bravado had carried her through the past two days, strengthening her to stand up to her father's disapproval, disarm her mother's worry, and laugh off her sister's fantasies. Thoughts bombarded her in a crazy mixture of excitement and nervousness. She had to succeed. She couldn't go back without her "Big Story."

She had no intention of failing. This was her most important assignment, even if she had delegated herself; and she'd write the best story of her career.

She opened her notebook and wrote in bold letters at the top of the page: "GERMANY, THE REAL STORY," then underneath, "by Amanda Chase."

A few lines lower she wrote: "HITLER—LIBERATOR OR TYRANT?" Too strong. She had no proof of the vague rumors she'd heard. Besides, reports touted him for miraculously bringing order and justice to the chaotic German politics and economy.

She crossed that headline out, and wrote "GERMANY, A MODERN-DAY UTOPIA" and a subtitle, "Or Does a Secret Shame Mar the Image?" She smiled. For now, that would do. She imagined a front-page headline, with inches and inches of story and a photograph beneath her byline.

She hung up her clothes in the small closet and folded her underwear in the dresser. Her Bible went on the nightstand. Slipping her book, *Guide to Germany,* in her purse, she left. It was time to meet people and find her roommate. There must be Germans on board, and she intended to meet and interview them.

❧

After seeing his wife and two daughters off, Amanda's father sat in his drawing room, drumming his fingers on the desk, thinking. Amanda had always been a dutiful, obedient daughter. Perhaps the philosophers were right—it wasn't a good idea to educate a girl too much. But she was bright, and he would have been wasteful to restrain her curious mind from exploring all the knowledge she craved.

He moved the inkwell a fraction of an inch, wondering if he should have introduced her to more young men; but he'd been proud when she devoured the business details of the galleries. If she'd been a son, she'd have followed in his footsteps and be running one of them now.

But she was a girl, and therefore had led a sheltered life. She'd always traveled with the family, and had no idea how dangerous traveling alone could be for a woman. He paced the room, grinding his teeth. *Should have forbidden the impetuous girl to go,* he thought. But he'd tried that, and she lifted her chin in defiance, stating she was free, grown-up, and was going.

He stared out the french doors. Reaching a decision, he strode back to his desk and picked up the phone.

❧

Curley and the crew relaxed as the powerful Boeing 247 flew high over the Atlantic Ocean toward England. After the sun set behind them the blackness was punctuated by stars above and a few weak lights from an occasional boat below.

Motioning to Jim Blake, his copilot, to take over, Curley pulled off his headphones and worked his way to the rear of the plane. He pulled a Coke from the ice cooler, popped off the cap, and took a long swallow. He glanced at his watch: 6:40 P.M. East Coast time. Smith, the other crew member, was stretched out across two of the airplane's seats, asleep.

Curley had been in the cockpit for hours and had no desire for more sitting, so he braced his arm above one of the windows and looked out. These same stars shone over California, where he'd be right now if his orders hadn't taken him east instead.

It had been almost two years since he'd been back west. He'd looked forward to surprising Johnny and Meredith when he flew his Moth onto their airstrip. But he'd have to wait.

A wispy cloud passed the window, disappearing like smoke. He dropped the empty Coke bottle into the box beside the ice chest and went to the other side to look out. Another gauzy cloud flew past, and he had to catch hold of the seat back to maintain his balance as the plane began to climb.

He made his way forward and got into his seat. Blake glanced at him. They were climbing through clouds and the turbulence jabbed at the plane, rocking them in their seats. Curley motioned to Blake to continue taking her up over the problem, while he grabbed the swaying flight chart off its peg and checked the instruments. They were 522 miles east of St. John's in Newfoundland.

The big plane bounced its way up, as if ascending stairs. For ten minutes both pilots fought to hold it steady. Suddenly a vicious blast of wind shoved them sideways, and the right wing dipped, dangerously threatening to send them into a stall.

"We can't climb out! Clouds too high," Curley yelled. "Let's take her down and see if it's better underneath."

They pushed the controls slowly forward, carefully maneuvering the plane down through the turbulence.

"Trouble on engine one," called Blake. Curley looked to his left. Through ice particles flying past, he saw small flames flickering behind the propellers.

"Hold on, baby," he murmured, and eased up on the throttles, enough to let the plane glide slightly, yet enough to maintain control. Smith had entered the cockpit, and stood, bracing his hands on the ceiling, watching the struggle against the buffeting winds.

According to the altimeter they were six hundred feet above water. "We'd better bottom out under this storm soon or we'll be in the drink," shouted Smith. With one last jolt as if they'd been spit out, they emerged from the cloud.

They turned southward, staying beneath the cloud, until they found its edge and rose again to higher altitude. Following their radio beacon, they were soon back on course.

They all three sighed in relief and began checking the damage, especially to engine number one. Smith went to the rear, while Blake and Curley checked electrical and pressure gauges.

"Manifold pressure is down," said Curley. Blake nodded. "We can't land and fix her," he added, "so we'd better start lightening our load."

"There's not much cargo back there, sir," said Blake, "but we can toss out seats and fixtures."

"You and Smith get on it, and I'll keep her steady."

"Yes, sir." Jim Blake disengaged himself from his seat and left the cockpit.

Curley shut the traitorous engine down, and feathered the propeller to keep the plane on a steady course with the one remaining engine. With over a thousand miles to go, even if they lightened the load, the chances of setting down in England were small. He considered turning back, but the chances of running into the storm behind them checked him.

He felt the surge of lightness as the crewmen reduced the load. When Blake and Smith returned he said, "One engine is damaged. The plane won't make it, not unless we lighten her load even more. Only two people are necessary to fly this baby, so as soon as we see a ship, one of us is going to book passage."

"I'm the heaviest," said Smith. "I volunteer."

Curley shook his head. "We're all checked out to fly her, so what we're going to do is draw straws to see who takes a cruise."

Blake pulled out three matches, broke one, and turned aside, arranging them in his fist. Smith pulled the first, a whole match, then Curley drew the short one. "But, sir. . ."

"That's the deal, and there's nothing to say," said Curley. "Now, when you get to Sedley Field, report what happened, and tell them I'll report in as soon as possible. Now let's hope the first ship we come across is a seaworthy vessel heading east."

Handing the controls to Smith, he went aft to secure his suitcase near the cargo door, and strapped on a parachute. He scanned the black water below, suddenly engulfed in the horrible image of water closing around him, crushing him. These disturbing anxieties surfaced occasionally, since the day his father's foreman had broken the news of his father's death in a collapsed Arizona cave. Curley was nine at the time. He shook off the gruesome vision, renewing his vow to avoid caves and dark underground chambers. Compared to that, jumping into the darkness below would be a breeze.

&

On deck, Amanda clutched the railing and hunched her shoulders against the cold wind. Ilsa, her redheaded Norwegian roommate, stood beside her. Ilsa had been curious about Amanda's ubiquitous notebook and pencil, and when she found out Amanda was a reporter, she appointed herself as her assistant. The same age as Victoria, Ilsa proved to be a cheerful companion.

"If my Uncle Eric were here, he'd say the wind is charged with the feel of a coming storm," said Ilsa.

"It's whipping up the water." The slap of waves against the side of the boat almost drowned out Amanda's reply. In the four days they'd been collaborating, they had investigated the ship, its operation and crew, and some passengers.

"I followed those two big fellas to the lounge this morning. They spent a lot of time in there. I think they're gangsters."

Amanda moved her hands away from the warm spot they'd made on the railing, then moved them back. "We could interview them and ask them."

"But, they wouldn't tell us! I think we should. . ."

". . .give those two wide berth," said Amanda. "I'm more interested in interviewing the Mexican acrobats who are going to entertain us tonight."

"Remember, you said I could come with you."

"Right. Now let's get back to our room and go over our list of questions."

That night, after the acrobats finished their show and two encores, Amanda and Ilsa interviewed them with the handsome purser there to translate. But the father of the talented family spoke some English, giving Amanda good quotes for a story.

While she was asking the age of the youngest girl, an ensign rushed in and urgently tapped the purser on the shoulder, telling him the captain wanted him right away.

Sniffing a story, Amanda quickly thanked the Escobar family and followed the purser to the bridge. Captain McNally and several of his crew held receivers to their ears, listening with great concentration. Amanda's eyes darted from one to the other, trying to figure out whether another ship was in trouble, or if dire world news was coming over the radio waves.

"We hear you, N-C-niner-five-five. Go ahead," the captain spoke into the ship-to-ship communications system.

Ilsa tiptoed to the purser and put a light hand on his shoulder. "What's happening?" she asked.

He shook his head and lifted his shoulders, a bewildered look on his face.

"Cut the engines," barked the captain, squinting out into the darkness. "All hands on deck. And spread out."

Amanda stepped back to let them by, then she followed. As soon as they stepped outside, they heard the drone of an approaching airplane.

four

Curley communicated to the ship's captain that they'd be overhead shortly. When they approached the ship, Smith said, "Good luck, sir, and don't get wet."

Curley grinned and patted the suitcase tied to his parachute harness. "Hey, in my barnstorming days I could jump from a thousand feet and land on a nickel."

Smith opened the passenger door. The lights of the ship came closer, and Curley shouted, "See you at Sedley." He pushed himself into the night air and relished the brief silence.

"One thousand. . .two thousand. . .three thousand. . . PULL!" His right arm reached across his chest, found the rip cord, and yanked. He felt the jerk and then the bobbling motion of the chute opening. He looked up in satisfaction at the white canopy overhead. Below, a ring of lights glowed on a cleared area near the ship's stern, and he settled into his harness, preparing for landing.

సా

Sensing a good story, Amanda raced down to her cabin and snatched up her camera and flashbulbs. She was back on deck in time to see four crewmen setting up a fifteen-foot circle of lights on the promenade deckhouse roof. A crowd had gathered, murmuring baffled comments as they watched the sailors.

Amanda spotted Ilsa on the roof, waving at her and tugging on the purser's sleeves. He gestured to the men at the bottom of the steps holding back the crowd, and they let Amanda by.

She snapped pictures of crewmen standing around the lighted area looking up. A large plane roared overhead and in a few seconds a chutist drifted toward them, his parachute a white dot in the dark sky. She focused on the man floating

33

down. But he was still only a white dot in her lens.

"I hope he doesn't land in the water!" cried Ilsa.

"If he's good, and if the wind is right, he'll land right here," said the purser, quickly looking away from Ilsa's shining eyes.

Amanda hoped this man was as skilled as some of the experts she'd seen at air shows. She watched, fascinated, as the man skillfully maneuvered directly over the lighted circle. She snapped his picture. He came closer. She popped a bulb in the flash in time to snap his feet hitting the deck. She shot another as his parachute drifted down around him, and he quickly gathered it up. The crowd on the deck below applauded.

Amanda's finger froze on the shutter release. She lowered the camera to get a better look. Curley Cameron! It was really him! She pulled her gaze away, aware that she was gawking. With trembling fingers she picked up the spent flashbulbs at her feet.

The crew had gathered around Curley, congratulating him as he loosed himself from the parachute harness. Ilsa pulled herself away from the purser and whispered to Amanda, "Oooh, would you look at him?!"

Amanda did look. She blushed, remembering back almost seven years. She had been seventeen. Her father had taken her to an air show near New York, where Curley Cameron was billed as "Curley the Kid—the young daredevil from the Wild West." He'd flown his plane in the most outrageous loops and madcap upside-down tricks, making her almost swoon with fright that he might crash, but afraid to tear her eyes away.

After the show, at a reception in her father's country club, she was introduced to him. He charmed her so thoroughly that later she haggled with a girl who'd bought his picture from a hawker and had brought it to the reception; Amanda finally persuaded her to trade the picture for Amanda's beaded purse. After that, she saved newspaper articles about him, and pinned them up in her dormitory room when she returned to school in Paris a month later.

That had been so long ago, a silly schoolgirl crush. She thought she'd forgotten the appealing young man with the dimpled smile. Apparently she hadn't. She gazed at him for a moment, noticing that the years had been good to him; he looked more handsome and rugged than the eighteen-year-old she remembered.

He still had a friendly face with eyes that seemed to have a perpetual teasing light in them. His dark red hair was combed back and trimmed neatly over his ears. As if drawn by a magnet, his eyes looked directly at her. She could feel a pulse throbbing in her neck, and she raised a hand to her throat as if to still it. Then he looked away and the moment passed.

"Oh, Amanda! He looked right at me!" Ilsa grabbed Amanda's sleeve. "Come on! Let's get closer."

Amanda dropped the spent bulbs into a sack in her camera bag. He hadn't recognized her. *Of course, why should he?* she asked herself. But still, an odd twinge of disappointment nudged her. She shook it off, coming back to reality.

"Amanda!" Ilsa's urgent tugging amused Amanda, reminding her of Victoria's methods of coercion. "This is a scoop! A big story," she added. "Come on!"

Amanda snapped her camera bag shut and followed Ilsa through the shipmen surrounding Curley. He had taken off his parachute and knelt as he packed it neatly together. As there was nothing more for the crew to do, they drifted away, back to their work, The captain, purser, and an engineer remained, talking with Curley, their backs to Amanda and Ilsa.

Ilsa tapped the purser on his shoulder. "Where's he from?" she whispered.

"Looks American," he said.

". . .and I'll debark at your first port. . ." Curley's gaze slid past the captain to Ilsa, then Amanda. He stood up, the smile in his eyes revealing his delight at seeing them. "And what part of the crew are these lovely ladies?"

The captain stood back and nodded at Amanda. "This is Miss Amanda Chase, passenger and reporter," he nodded at Ilsa, "and this is Miss Ilsa Johnson, passenger and Ambassador of Cheer."

"Pleased to meet you both," he said, dipping his head slightly.

Amanda's jaw dropped in surprise for a second, before she could catch her breath. He was taller than she'd remembered, at least six-foot-three, somehow more athletic-looking, with wide shoulders looking as hard as granite beneath his flight suit.

The captain gestured with his hand to Curley. "And I'd like to introduce you to Curley Cameron, our newest passenger."

Ilsa eagerly reached out her hand, but instead of a formal handshake, Curley gave it a gentle squeeze. He glanced at Amanda for a second, then gave Ilsa a smile that made her grin and lift her shoulders in a childlike gesture of delight.

"No need to stand out here in the cold," said the captain, leading them toward the steps. Amanda clutched her sweater closer, realizing that the night wind had become chilly.

She couldn't think of a good reason to follow them, but she smelled a story too good to pass up. A few of the passengers who had lingered congratulated Curley as they walked toward the cabin-class promenade. One woman thanked the captain for the splendid show and asked why he hadn't announced it the day before so more passengers could enjoy it. Curley grinned and said he was glad she'd enjoyed it. As they walked on, he winked at Amanda and Ilsa, as though they shared a private joke.

Amanda boldly met his eyes, denying to herself the feeling that the temperature had just gone up ten degrees. She looked away, mentally concentrating on a headline: *The Man Who Dropped From the Sky.* Yes, that might do.

The ship shuddered as its great gears were engaged, moving forward again through the sea toward its first stop in France. Clutching the camera bag strap, Amanda braced her feet to steady herself. But there seemed no way to steady her mixed emotions.

Amanda and Ilsa stopped at the corridor to their cabin, and the men paused to wish them a good night.

"Mr. Cameron, I'd like to talk with you about your flying and parachuting adventures, if I may," said Amanda.

"It would be my pleasure," he answered.

They made arrangements to meet for breakfast the next morning before her ten o'clock interview with a baroness.

In the hallway back to their room, Ilsa danced in front of Amanda, skipping backward. "Let's go to the lounge. I'm too wound up to turn in!" she squeaked.

"You go on ahead. I have to plan my interview with the redoubtable Mr. Cameron."

"Plan? Don't be silly! Just ask whatever comes into your head."

"Goodness, no! I have to think of all the possible directions the interview could go, and be prepared."

"Well, if you must," said Ilsa with her hands on her hips, and shaking her head, "go ahead, but at least come when you're through. I'll save a place for you."

Amanda sighed. "I might, but don't get your hopes up." Before Ilsa rounded the corner behind her, Amanda had pulled out her notepad and was scribbling: *What were you doing up there? Why did you parachute out? Did you have to? Why in the middle of the Atlantic Ocean? Was the plane in trouble?* By the time she got back to her room, she already had half a dozen questions.

She sat, looking out the porthole to the silver-lined clouds, reminding herself that she was grown-up now. After all these years, the great Curley Cameron held no more appeal. Besides, he had obviously changed. That thought took her in the dangerous direction of his more manly, stronger appearance that made him infinitely more handsome and desirable than ever. *Headline, headline,* she told herself. *Airline Passenger Prefers Ocean Liner Luxury.* Too long. She couldn't concentrate.

❧

Curley settled himself in the small cabin on a lower deck, and stowed his flight suit in the bottom of his suitcase. What a day! He'd have to write to Johnny and Meredith to tell them that their prayers were working. They never failed to mention they were praying for him. *Well,* he thought, *this was one time I really needed it. If the ship hadn't been right in our path, and if the storm had covered more area than we'd thought, or if—*

He shook his head free of the negative thoughts and looked around the cabin. One room with a bunk, a desk and chair, a small closet with a dresser inside it, and a rest room just big enough to turn around in. He wouldn't spend much time in here anyway, because on the other side of the door was one great big ship to explore. The purser had given him a chart of the accommodations.

He set his suitcase inside the closet, then picked up the chart and went out to find if there was somewhere to get a bite to eat at ten o'clock. He found a small bar on B deck, where passengers in "lesser accommodations" gathered to socialize.

He ordered a roast beef sandwich and a Coke, and sat on a stool watching a young couple swaying together on the small dance floor. A plaintive song tinkled from the player piano in the corner. *This is probably their honeymoon voyage,* he thought.

He took a swig of Coke and narrowed his eyes, thinking. He'd have to get out of the interview with that reporter girl. The expression in her eyes when he looked up from his parachute startled him. He'd felt the strangest glimmer of recognition, something familiar about her he couldn't place. But that couldn't be. He'd never have forgotten a girl like her. But there was something, and it bothered him.

Too bad she was a reporter. A journalist was like a dog after a bone going for an interview. If she was reporting the story for some shipboard chronicle, it would be harmless, but if the story were to somehow get into the *real* newspapers, it could mean trouble for his mission. Since he couldn't dodge her forever, maybe he could invent some boring story that wouldn't capture her interest.

The piano stopped playing, and the young husband sauntered over to start a new tune. As Curley idly watched, he overheard a man speculating with the bartender why a man would parachute onto the ship. He had to reconsider letting the girl interview him, he realized; it would be too difficult to make his story boring.

☙

Though she was tempted, Amanda decided that bringing Ilsa to her interview with Curley would be cowardly. He couldn't know that she'd idolized him, even if he did remember her. So, arriving alone at the twelve-foot high double doors of the fashionable cabin-class dining saloon, she asked the steward to escort her to Curley's table. The aromas of coffee, freshly baked rolls, and eggs floated around Amanda, reminding her she was very hungry.

Curley held the chair for her, then sat across from her. "I'm starving. How about interviewing after we eat?"

His smile disarmed her nervousness, and she set her notebook and purse aside. "I wouldn't want to have to write the obituary of a man who starved to death giving an interview."

"Good." Curley glanced up into her eyes, entranced by the mixed shades of amber and green ringed by black lashes, and felt another strange glimmer of recognition. Something in her manner was vaguely disturbing. *Why is she looking at me like that?*

The waiter poured coffee for them and took their order. She asked him about his work, and he told her about his love of flying. She told him about newspaper reporting.

He asked her where she was going, and she told him of her aunt and uncle in Eisenburg. She glanced at the tables nearby to be sure no one was eavesdropping. "Mr. Hitler is getting so much good publicity these days, it makes one wonder how much of it is true." She lowered her voice and leaned forward. "I have sources that indicate otherwise."

He leaned forward and matched her soft voice. "Sounds like a daring adventure!"

Amanda sat up stiffly, feeling she might have revealed too much. "Oh, no. I've gone all over to get a story—even some very scary places." She sipped her coffee to capture her composure, and asked, "So, what's your business in Europe?"

"Are we officially starting the interview?" he asked.

"Might as well." She pulled a pencil from her purse, and picked up her tablet. Flipping the cover to her page of questions, she read the first one: "What is your full name?"

"Curley Cameron, at your service, ma'am."

She paused and looked up at him. "Is Curley the name on your birth certificate?"

"No, but I've been called Curley as long as I can remember, and it fits me better than the other, more proper names."

"Well, it'll do, I guess. So, Mr. Cameron. . ."

"Curley."

"So, Curley, where were you headed when you found yourself directly over this ocean liner?"

His eyes caught and held hers, which she found vaguely disturbing. "You're asking which direction I was going?"

"Yes."

"To Europe, same as you. How long have your aunt and uncle lived in Eisenburg?"

"I'm the one doing the interviewing."

He cocked his eyebrows and shrugged his shoulders. "Okeydokey."

His reaction amused her. "Aunt Esther and Uncle Jacob have been in Eisenburg for eight years while they've been operating my father's art gallery. Were you one of the flight crew on that plane?"

"In a manner of speaking."

"Please elaborate." She looked at him, waiting for his answer.

"Look," he said, "maybe I want to know where my story and picture are going to appear. Who do you work for?"

She nodded. "A fair question. I work for the *Boston*

Chronicle. That's where I'll send the story."

"Hmm." His dark eyebrows slanted in a frown as he considered this. Suddenly, as if the sunshine overcame the darkening doubts, his lips turned up in a grin, and he nodded. "All right."

His appealing smile almost made her forgot her questions. She stared at him, unable to say a word.

"How about if I just tell you what happened, and you can ask what you want when I'm through."

She nodded. "Fine. Begin."

"I was one of a crew of men bringing the new Boeing 247 to England, when we hit a storm north of here. One of our engines was damaged and we had to lighten the load. Finally one of us had to abandon the plane. This vessel was the first one we contacted, and luckily it wasn't going west. We contacted the captain, and here I am."

Amanda listened and made notes. The story seemed too smooth somehow, too convenient. He was leaving something out. "Were there passengers aboard?"

"No. How long are you going to be in Eisenburg?" He watched her with great interest, and she had to fight an impulse to lean closer toward him. *What a frustrating man!* He was distracting her from probing further into his story.

She clenched her jaw, and wrote the headline, "Abandon Plane!" circling it. Keeping her tone even, she asked, "Who do you work for?"

He stood. "I wouldn't want to make any bad publicity for my bosses, now would I?" He came around the table and stood behind her chair, ready to pull it out when she stood.

Amanda made no attempt to stand. She stubbornly held her notebook up with the pencil poised over it. He leaned over her shoulder and said softly, "We can continue out on the deck." Her cheek grew warm where his breath softly fanned it. She didn't dare turn her head; his face was too close to hers. She was more tempted than offended.

Snapping her notebook shut, she grabbed her purse, and stood. He held the chair out for her, and with his hand under her elbow, guided her out of the elegant dining room.

I used to dream of being with him, she thought. *But in my dreams he was mellower, more agreeable. Reality is like having a wildcat by the tail.* She fought the impulse to walk away, yet she didn't want to lose a good story.

five

The feel of Curley's hand on her arm warmed Amanda as they walked out into the sunshine. A fresh, salt-scented breeze fanned them as they made their way across the gently rolling deck, passing other passengers who didn't recognize Curley as the man who had parachuted from the sky the night before. In his dark pants, blue shirt, and pullover sweater, Amanda thought he looked more the college man than daredevil.

He steered her around a maid walking two little prancing dogs and said, "What drew you to newspaper writing?"

She looked away from his dimpled grin. "It's my way of helping people understand what's happening in this world."

"Ah, yes. The trip to Germany." They stepped close to the rail as a group of children trooped by, herded by a buxom young woman wearing sturdy shoes. She nodded to Amanda, glanced at Curley, and dropped her gaze, then shouted to the children to keep up with her. She was the ship's junior activity organizer. Amanda had interviewed her on her first day aboard. Though she looked like a girl, the young woman was twenty-nine years old.

"So, where were we?" asked Curley.

She opened her notebook to a blank page. "We were talking about careers. So, what made you decide to fly airplanes?" Her thoughts traveled back to his wild air show escapades. It was on the tip of her tongue to tell him that she'd seen him then, but she decided not to. Maybe later, when she got to know him a little better.

He looked out over the sea, squinting at the billowy clouds on the horizon and lifted his shoulders. "It's something I always knew I'd do." He turned and leaned back, resting his elbows on the railing. "Hung around airplanes till I was old enough to fly. I took to the air as naturally as I breathe."

She forced herself to look away from his dimpled smile and his hazel eyes that danced with life and mischief. "I know exactly what you mean," she said, jotting his statement in her notebook.

Curley watched her write, enjoying her nearness. Though he enjoyed women in general, this one intrigued him, with her hypnotic eyes the same green color as the sea. She was exquisitely beautiful, like a soft ribbon of moonlight glowing on the tops of clouds. He never forgot a face, and he knew he'd met her somewhere. It bothered him that he couldn't remember. He'd never had to resort to the old line of asking a girl if they'd met before. He was beginning to think this was the time.

They stood there for a few minutes, while he answered her questions and peppered the conversation with a few of his own.

Amanda's pulse was racing and she bit her lip to force herself to concentrate on the interview. A middle-aged man in a bad mood and a suit too large asked if they'd seen the steward. They hadn't, so he grumbled and went to look for him.

She'd asked Curley all her questions, and there was nothing more to say. But she didn't want the interview to end. She looked at her watch and gasped. It was 9:45.

"What's the matter? Coaches don't turn into pumpkins until midnight," he said, devastating her with that smile again.

She snapped her notebook shut with the pencil inside and shoved it into her purse. "I have to interview a baroness in fifteen minutes."

"Time not only passes, it flies sometimes, doesn't it?"

Amanda smiled, feeling comfortable with him. "Definitely."

Curley drew in a deep, shaky breath and guided her across the white scrubbed boards, past the linoleum stairway, down to the second-class deck, to the elevators. Each elevator had a bas-relief motif signifying its destination. The library elevator had open books over the door, a smoking cigar noted the smoking lounge. The one to the swimming pool was adorned with mermaids and shells. She entered that one, and he held the door open.

He leaned inside. "I'd like to escort you to the banquet and ball tonight. What do you say?"

He looked like a hopeful teenager asking for his first date. "You haven't finished the interview," he added.

She felt a strange tugging on her heart. "All right. That would be nice."

Curley grinned and let the filigreed door shut. He liked a decisive woman. "I'll be at your cabin at 8:00," he said, raising his head to follow the elevator's upwards glide.

Her few words, "But you don't know my. . ." were lost in her ascent. He stood, looking up with a happy grin on his face. "Don't worry. I'll find you." The library elevator landed with a thunk. Curley smiled and whistled a tune as he passed the opening door.

&

Amanda hurried to the heated pool, where the baroness and her personnel occupied the stern end of the pool. The water faintly lapped against the blue and gold mosaic tiles. At the other end a waterfall cascaded over a series of lighted steps that made the water sparkle as it fell. A few swimmers were enjoying the pool, while some sat sipping champagne and showing off their French designer bathing suits.

Amanda took in the atmosphere, and stored it in her memory for story background. She approached the baroness, who was as slim as a fashion model and attired in an elegant black cape over her silver bathing suit.

&

After the interview, Amanda went back to her room and raised the blinds the maid had shut. Ilsa had been there and changed clothes. What she'd worn at breakfast was carelessly tossed on her bed. Amanda smiled, thinking of Victoria, and sat at the writing desk to compose her notes and impressions before she forgot them. She gazed out at the darkening clouds and composed headlines. *Baroness Bares All*. . . No maybe not; she giggled, thinking someone might get the wrong idea, and wrote a few more titles.

Soon it was time to meet Ilsa for tea. She folded her notes

and put them in a large envelope and wrote "Baroness" on it, then freshened up in the bathroom and left.

In the Grand Lounge Ilsa sat at a table near a bank of palm fronds. With her sat a tall, very handsome blond man dressed in white pants and striped shirt. He stood and pulled Amanda's chair out for her.

Ilsa's eyes sparked with delight as she introduced Nels Thordahl. His white eyelashes fringed sapphire blue eyes. "I am so glad to meet you," he replied with a Scandinavian accent, vigorously shaking her hand.

Ilsa could barely contain her excitement. "Nels won a tennis championship, next year he might play in Wimbledon, he's from Bergen, close to my hometown, and—"

Amanda had to laugh at the expression on Nels's face. He was nodding in agreement, and he didn't take his eyes off Ilsa.

Amanda declined the turtle soup the waiter offered, choosing cucumber sandwiches and a spoonful of cashew nuts instead. She glanced across the lounge, but didn't see Curley. On the bandstand a clarinetist stood, performing his solo part as the small band played "Bye, Bye Blackbird."

Ilsa and Nels continued to describe the beauties of Norway and Amanda promised to visit someday.

Though happy for Ilsa, who'd said she wanted a shipboard romance, Amanda felt like an old-maid aunt at their party. A short, dainty woman in a shiny pink dress passed their table, followed by a middle-aged man with dark wavy hair. The woman's strappy shoes matched her dress. This woman would be a knockout at the Grand Ball, and Amanda wondered which of her two evening dresses she should wear.

As if Ilsa had read her mind, she said, "Nels is going to be our escort to the ball tonight!"

Amanda smiled into their eager faces, and said, "How gallant! But, I have an escort, thank you." A vision of Curley's boyish grin between the elevator doors brought a warm glow to her cheeks.

Ilsa sat straight up in her chair, almost knocking off the tray of hot scones, strawberry preserves, and clotted cream the waiter was placing on their table. "Who? Who? No! Let me guess!" She gazed upward and frowned thoughtfully, then beamed with delight. "The man from the sky! Right?"

"Right." Amanda glanced at her watch. "I have a lot of things to do between now and then, so I'll see you later, at the cabin." Nels quickly rose and moved her chair back for her.

❧

Amanda chose her dusky rose satin dress with a ruffled collar that dipped low in the back. Ilsa wore black. They stood side by side before the green marble counter in their bathroom. Amanda patted loose powder on her nose, while Ilsa leaned forward to stroke pink lipstick on her pursed lips.

Pulling on her earlobe, Amanda winced. "I shouldn't have let you talk me into buying these earrings. This one pinches!"

"Here, let me fix it for you."

Amanda unclipped it, just as someone rapped on their door. She went to answer it while Ilsa concentrated on bending the earring wire to loosen it.

Amanda opened the door and gasped. Curley stood in the hallway, in a black tuxedo made of some soft-looking material, over a pleated white shirt with a black tie at his neck. Abruptly, she dropped her gaze, embarrassed to be caught staring, and invited him in. She caught the masculine scent of his cologne as he passed her.

Curley crossed the threshold into definitely feminine territory, and held out a white gardenia corsage. He breathed deeply. "It smells nice in here." The room smelled like a rose and lavender garden, mingled now with the scent of gardenia.

Ilsa came out from the bathroom with the earring. "Hello, again," she said to Curley.

"Hello." He gulped to quell the dizzy sensation racing through him as Amanda in her shimmery floor-length gown fastened the gardenia to her dress. Most of her thick dark hair was piled high on her head, with a cascade of curls laying against her creamy skin. He was entranced by the graceful way her hands moved as she tilted her head and clipped on the earring.

She picked up her beaded bag. Another visitor knocked on the door and Ilsa started toward it. She stopped, lifted her head in dignified control, and walked slowly to answer it.

The four of them stepped off the elevator into a chattering crowd in the grand lounge. Some of the gowns were elegant, some scandalously revealing, and all very expensive. Jewels glittered everywhere. One woman had a diamond necklace so large it lay over her bosom like a sparkling bib.

A deep gong echoed through the room, announcing that the banquet was served. Curley escorted Amanda into the first-class dining saloon. The diners' entrance was like a grand procession. The orchestra played a lush Jerome Kern melody, with cymbals and trumpets punctuating the violins. The baroness entered, looking regal in a slim evening gown of gold lace. Her retinue strode behind her, in the wake of her grandeur. She and one of her companions separated themselves from the group and went to the captain's table.

Ilsa and Nels found their table, then Curley guided Amanda to the captain's table, where he pulled out a chair for her. She nodded to acknowledge the baroness, and sat down. The man across from her looked like an aging movie star. He dominated the conversation with a story about a recent safari in Africa.

After the appetizers were cleared away, the stewards scurried around the table with dove breasts in ginger-flavored aspic. The woman with the aging actor took up a lull in his conversation and leaned toward Curley. "I didn't catch your name?" she said. Her neckline dipped dangerously low.

Amanda turned her head to avoid the view, and Curley kept his eyes riveted on the woman's face. He nodded toward Amanda and said, "Amanda Chase. And I'm James Cameron."

"Sit back, darling." The actor gently touched her bare shoulder, and she relaxed in her seat with a petulant frown on her pretty lips.

"What do you do, Mr. Cameron?" asked the man.

"Oh, a little of this and a little of that," shrugged Curley. "Nothing as exciting and courageous as your exploits."

The man leaned sideways slightly so the steward could

remove one plate and place another before him. With a bored look he answered, "It gets tiresome sometimes, and one longs for home and hearth. You know?"

"Have you ever been to Poland?" asked Curley.

This set the man off on another story that lasted through the main course, sorbet, and into dessert.

Amanda longed to ask the man if he was an actor, but decided that if he was, she should know his name, and if he was nobility or a wealthy businessman, he'd be offended. She smiled at his lovely companion, who kept glancing at Curley with a hungry look. Curley nodded at the right places in the man's story and seemed interested, but the moment Amanda glanced at him, he winked at her and reached beneath the table to grasp her hand.

She took a deep breath to maintain her poise, but a stir of something deep in her heart pushed her emotions off balance. She looked down the table, catching the eye of the baroness, who raised her eyebrows inquisitively.

At last the dinner was over and the crowd made its way to the grand ballroom. Curley put his hand on Amanda's slim waist and guided her through the moving stream of people. When the guests turned right, he steered her to the left, toward a balcony-type landing with an arched window. A cool ocean breeze drifted in from the black sky and ocean.

He put his hands on her upper arms, and in the shadowy light his features softened. He looked too good to be true. *No wonder the woman across the table from us couldn't keep her eyes off him*, thought Amanda. He was one of those rare men who could dress up and look more masculine than ever.

"Why didn't you tell that man that you're a flier?" she asked. "Especially when he told the story about flying over the Yukon snows to hunt moose?"

Curley chuckled. "He was blowing smoke. You know, telling a yarn. Why rain on the guy's parade? Especially when he's the grand marshal!"

"You skillfully evaded my detailed questions about your flying. There's some reason you don't want to talk about it.

You're not shy, are you?" She grimaced, reaching up to unclip her left earring, and rubbed her sore earlobe. He looked so concerned she smiled back at him. "New earrings," she explained.

He gazed so long at her, watching her closely, that she turned her head in embarrassment. He gently reached out, touched her chin, and turned her head toward him. "I know this may sound like a come-on, but I've met you somewhere before."

Her heart skipped a beat, and she wanted to turn her head away, but she continued to gaze back at him.

He looked past her, out to the black night. "Somewhere, I know it." His eyes focused back on her. "Or maybe it was only in my dreams."

His thumb slowly caressed her arm, and she tried to still her response to the tingling feeling racing through her. She licked her lips. "Actually, we, umm. . ."

His hand slid up to the back of her neck and he drew her toward him, murmuring, "Actually we're here right now, and . . ." His face drew nearer to hers. "And you're more beautiful than any dream I've ever had."

Amanda closed her eyes as the distance between them vanished, and he kissed her.

The warmth of his lips on hers sparked a response that surprised her. She started to raise her hands to lay them on the smooth white shirt front, then stopped herself. As much as she wanted to resist, she found herself rising on her tiptoes, eagerly responding to the delicious sensations she was feeling.

She basked in the glow for a long moment, then realized he wasn't kissing her anymore. Her eyes flew open to see him gazing at her in wonder. He was close, so close she longed to reach up and pull his head down and continue what they'd started. Somewhere inside her a voice warned against letting her feelings control her.

As if sensing her reluctance, he drew back slightly, but he didn't stop staring down at her.

"You," he breathed. "It's so. . .I mean. . ." For once, Curley was at a loss for words. He couldn't tear his gaze away from the moist gentleness of her mouth, the large, soft eyes that showed too much what she was feeling. He'd kissed enough women to know she wanted him to kiss her again, but he was disturbed by the fierce desire that rose up in him to do exactly that.

He framed her face with both of his hands and said, "Are you real, or am I dreaming?" She slowly closed her eyes, interrupting the strong force transmitted through their eyes.

Struggling for control, Amanda stood still, trying to make sense out of what had just happened. But wonderful warm waves of pleasure washing through her made it difficult to think clearly.

He grinned down at her and said, "It's pretty heady stuff out here. Would you like to go see how the other half is celebrating? There's a party on each level."

She nodded, not trusting herself to say a word.

"Come on, then." He held out his hand, and she laid hers in it, allowing him to lead her to the lower levels of the ship.

In the second-class salon, with its dark paneling showing off floral bouquets in lighted, window-size recessed frames, the passengers were slow dancing to soft music. Curley and Amanda found a table and ordered lemon-lime fizzes. A bowl of chocolate mints and peanuts sat beside a small candle lamp set in the middle of the pink linen tablecloth.

Curley leaned forward and put his hand over hers. "At last I've got you all to myself," he said. He raised his eyes. "Up there, too many people, too much distraction."

Amanda smiled, thinking that being on a real date with her hero, Curley Cameron, was a dream she'd given up ever coming true. But here she was, and it was happening. "I'll let you off the hook tonight," she said, removing the earrings that were still pinching. "But tomorrow we land in France, and it'll be a madhouse from then until we dock in London."

"I'll never be off your hook, Amanda Chase," said Curley. He picked up one of the chocolate mints and slowly held it up to her mouth. She laughed and called him silly, and he slipped the chocolate inside.

Amanda let the sweet dark flavor melt on her tongue for a moment, then said, "I'm going to the church service tomorrow morning. Let's finish the interview right after, all right?"

He smiled and it was as intimate as a caress. "No business tonight. Save a place for me in church. I'll meet you there, then we'll talk."

She studied him thoughtfully for a moment. "Are you a believer?"

"Yes!" he exclaimed, his face shining with glad memories. "I vaguely remember my mother praying, but then she died and my dad and I never went to church. When I was older I met up with some Christians who took me in, gave me a job, and," he shrugged, "God sort of snuck up on me." He shook his head. "No, He was always there, so trusting Him was the most natural thing in the world."

Amanda felt a warm glow settle over her.

Curley stood and grabbed her hand. She slipped her earrings into his tuxedo pocket and followed him.

They went deeper down to the third-class saloon. The air was thick with smoke, and passengers snaked through the room, stepping and swaying to some line dance. The revelers looked so silly to Amanda that she laughed, partly at the scene before her but mostly for the sheer joy of being with Curley.

They stood in the doorway, watching. Curley waved his hands before his face. "If I had a knife, I could cut a path through the smoke so we could enter." He glanced at her, enjoying the sparkle of her smile and her infectious laugh. He chuckled and, with his hand on her elbow, led her back into the hallway.

They climbed to the upper levels, passing a few people at a distance. He'd loosened his tie, and she clung to his arm while they strolled along the deck beside the rail, looking out over the water and talking. The musical hum of the engines and the gentle dip and roll of the deck cradled them in a special moment in time on the Atlantic waters. They told each other of their childhoods, their families, compared likes and dislikes, and found that they had a lot of attitudes and opinions in common.

Curley noticed that there were fewer and fewer people out on the deck, and the ship seemed to glide more quietly through the black swells. He'd never felt so comfortable with a woman, and he didn't want the moment to end. He saw her suppress small shivers, so he put his arm around her as they leaned out over the rail, watching the foam lap against the ship's wall. "Let's stay here and talk all night," he said. "I've never met anyone so easy to talk to."

Amanda watched a sliver of moon lifting from the black horizon. "Your childhood is truly fascinating. It's sad that you were orphaned at such a young age, but the way you followed your dream of flight, making a home in the hangars and eventually with a mechanic. . . ." She looked at his strong profile watching the same moonrise. "It's like dime novel stories of a boy running away to join the circus."

He caught her gaze. "It wasn't all as exciting as it sounds." The corners of his mouth lifted in a slight smile. "But I did eventually perform in air circuses."

Amanda opened her mouth to tell him she'd seen him perform, but before she got the chance he said, "I wish you could have seen my aerobatics. But since the government cracked down on daredevils, we've had to find other ways to get our thrills in the sky."

"Like parachuting onto ships at sea?" Her eyes glowed with speculation in the pale moonlight, and Curley shook his head slowly. "That's the business part, which we'll discuss later."

"Later," she agreed.

"Meanwhile, let's get you back to your cabin for a catnap so you don't fall asleep in church tomorrow."

They strolled slowly back to her cabin, neither one wanting the evening to end. Curley kept a protective arm over her shoulder. "You know," he said, "you're a courageous woman, and I admire that."

"Me? I'm merely working for what I feel is right."

"Not all women would go to such lengths to try to make

sense of this crazy world. You're like a missionary."

They stopped at her cabin door. "My mission is to find the truth and reveal it to the world, so people can form their own opinions."

"Well said! If you ever run for president, I'll vote for you."

She loved the amusement that flickered in his eyes and the companionship they shared. As she watched, the amusement began to disappear and a contemplative look came into his hazel eyes.

She thought for a moment he was going to kiss her, but he said, "Be careful, Princess. Don't trust everything you see in Germany to be as it seems."

"But that's why I'm going!" she said with a smile.

He lifted his brows in acceptance, and said, "Just remember. Be careful."

"I'm always careful." She put her hand on the door handle. "Good night, then. And thanks for a wonderful evening."

He quickly brushed his lips over hers and came away with his eyes half closed. "Thank *you*," he said. She watched him walk away, then she slipped inside the dark cabin. She closed the door softly and leaned against it with a sigh.

❧

Curley felt like skipping, but he settled for a fast trot back to his cabin. A note hastily stuck to his cabin door caught his attention. "Contact Captain McNally immediately." He stuck the note into his pocket and loped down the silent hallway.

A crewman ushered him into the bridge. "The captain has retired for the night, but he asked us to wake him when you arrived." He nodded to the crewman standing at the wheel. "I'll return shortly," he told him. Passing Curley on his way out, he said, "We tried to locate you, but. . ."

Curley locked his hands behind his waist and looked around. In contrast to a cockpit, the bridge seemed spacious. Rows of shiny dials lined one wall, and a gyrocompass and electric telegraph stood against the other.

The crewman at the wheel noted his interest and said, "The very latest equipment."

"She's a fine ship indeed," agreed Curley. He squinted at one dial. "This looks like a wind velocity indicator."

"Right. The latest in anemometers."

He was about to say more, but Captain McNally came in, followed by his crewman. The captain was in uniform and looked as if he were rested and ready to face the day. He reached into a drawer near his chair and pulled out a piece of paper. "This came over the telegraph at oh-one-hundred." He handed it to Curley.

"Captain James Lee Cameron. USN dispatching ship to intercept and retrieve. ETA 0400 hrs." He stared at it for a moment, trying to make sense of it. Why? He planned to dock in France, find an airfield, then report to Sedley in England.

Captain McNally interrupted his musings. "Captain Campbell, you have exactly forty-two minutes to get your gear together and report back here."

Hurrying back to his cabin, Curley struggled to think of a way he could explain his leaving to Amanda. The retrieval ship was obviously coming at an hour which was meant to keep the rendezvous a secret from the passengers. What would she think when he didn't show up in church? He didn't have to guess. She'd think he was a playboy, who was merely toying with her.

He yanked the few clothes from the hangers in the closet and stuffed them into his suitcase. What were his intentions toward Amanda? He shook his head in consternation. Maybe he'd never know. But he'd have liked to have known her better.

He glanced at his watch. He had about five minutes leeway to dash to Amanda's cabin and—and what? He couldn't tell her anything without arousing wild suspicions. And he didn't even have time to tell her he wouldn't be at church.

When he arrived back at the bridge a few minutes later, the navy ship's lights were approaching. He asked Captain McNally for a slip of paper, and scribbled a short note. "Please see that Miss Amanda Chase in Cabin A-12 gets this message."

six

Amanda awoke the next morning with the pleasant feeling of lingering, nice dreams. As she surfaced up through the sleepy fog she realized that the images were real. She'd spent the most romantic evening of her life with the man of her young dreams.

Young dreams, she thought. A wonderful gift from her guardian angel. She inhaled deeply and opened her eyes. On the other bed Ilsa lay curled beneath her covers, clutching her extra pillow to her chest.

Amanda turned to lie on her back and gaze up at the polished wooden ceiling. "Amanda's Idyllic Evening." It would make a good headline. She blocked out a full-page photo layout complete with captions describing the lovely scenes.

She allowed herself a few minutes of fantasizing, then got herself in hand. *You've daydreamed long enough. Time for reality!* She picked up her Bible and read for a few minutes, but had difficulty concentrating. The small clock ticking away on the table between the two beds said only 9:00. She closed her eyes. *Last night was nice,* she told herself, *but a romantic moonlit evening, party-going aboard a gently rolling ship, and a charming, handsome escort are nothing to go gaga over.* Not enough to make a girl lose her objectivity.

Remember Lili, she told herself. A French girl at the Sorbonne, Lili had fallen in love aboard ship and spent the whole school term crying over a man who never contacted her again. *None of that for me,* vowed Amanda. *No man is going to tip my life into a morass of tears.*

She tossed off the covers, rejected the image of Curley's dimpled face smiling at her, threatening to unravel all her fine logic, and padded into the bathroom. She ran warm water into the bathtub, keeping busy to avoid daydreams.

At 10:30 a steward brought a silver service with coffee and flaky rolls. Amanda poured herself coffee and said, "I'm going to skip breakfast and have brunch later, after church." She didn't tell Ilsa that she was busy controlling the butterflies in her stomach and trying to quench the excitement of seeing Curley.

"Me, too," answered Ilsa, lying in bed until the last possible minute while Amanda sipped her coffee. Neither noticed the note slipped between the sugar and creamer.

They left the room, passing early morning deck strollers. The instant they turned the corner toward the Garden Lounge, Nels hurried toward them, a large toothy smile lighting up his face. He held out a hand to each of them, and Amanda couldn't help but smile in return, avoiding the urge to let her glance slide off him to search for a certain auburn-haired fellow.

"You ladies look lovely this morning," he said in his lilting Norwegian accent.

They thanked him, and Amanda allowed herself to glance around at the people arriving for church while Ilsa chattered, "It's hard to believe the voyage is almost over."

"Ya," agreed Nels. "We leave America Monday, and come to France on Sunday. So fast a world!"

Two gentlemen in their gray morning coats and gray silk neckties nodded at them as they passed.

"Should we wait for Curley?" asked Ilsa.

"No, let's go on in. He'll find us," said Amanda, thinking that Curley could perhaps already be inside, saving them places.

Amanda sang the familiar hymns, and tried to concentrate on the speaker without turning to look behind her to see if Curley had come in. She finally reached into her purse for her small notebook, and forced herself to listen to the speaker by jotting down his main points. "Ambassadors for Christ," was the headline she gave his sermon. He reminded his listeners that no matter where they traveled, they'd always be God's ambassadors.

When she was thirteen years old Amanda's nanny, Miss Whitney, took her regularly to church. Amanda had had the

zeal of an ambassador then. But as she got busier with school
and traveling, she attended less often, except when accompa-
nying her parents to the cathedral's fashionable Christmas
and Easter services. But in the last two years she'd gone back
to church, seeking fellowship and stability.

After the closing hymn, Amanda, Ilsa, and Nels followed
the crowd out onto the deck.

"I wonder where Curley is," said Ilsa, frowning and looking about.

"Must have had better things to do," said Amanda, forcing
a smile. A high stack of cumulus clouds had risen and was
approaching like a white and gray army.

"Well! It's quite rude!" Ilsa glared at the back of a man
walking by, as if he were the guilty party. "It would be so
lovely to explore Cherbourg together this afternoon."

Amanda looked out over the deck rail to the dark green
cliffs in the distance. "Yes, it would be. You two go on ahead.
I have a million things to do before I arrive in England tomorrow." Before they could urge her to join them for brunch, she
added, "I have a couple more people to interview before we
dock. See you two later!"

Amanda turned and escaped to the other side of the ship,
spending the next two hours on a padded wooden deck chair
in an out-of-the-way corner on A deck. *I must remember that
this is not a pleasure trip,* she told herself, and began jotting
her thoughts on paper. *I can never allow myself to forget
those small stories buried in the newspapers—skeptical stories of outrageous rumors too horrible to believe. One writer
of such a story was forced to leave Germany. Persecution and
cruelty were never the central theme of stories of Hitler's new
regime. They mostly centered around the new orderly stability.*

She couldn't think of any more to add to her notes. She
simply had to get there, and assure herself that Aunt Esther,
Uncle Jacob, and her cousins were all right.

Quick, confident steps approached, and her heart beat a little faster, thinking that Curley had found her. A smile locked
itself on her mouth.

She blushed at her stupidity when a steward walked briskly past. *Captain Cameron means nothing to me,* she told herself. *But, what if something came up, and he's looking for you right this moment? What if he's sick, or if he was waylaid by. . .*

She leapt up from the chair, and stomped off the deck, and down a linoleum stairway. *Sure. He was kidnapped by pirates. If Captain Curley Cameron, or CCC, as she began thinking of him, were really interested in you, he would have been where he said he'd be. So, face it!* she told herself.

Two long, majestic blasts of the ship's whistle drowned out her footsteps as she entered the second-class lounge. She found a table near the porthole and munched on cashew nuts, watching small boats bobbing in the distance as the big liner cruised into the harbor.

After the ship docked and those passengers who were going ashore left, Amanda made her way back to her cabin.

🙵

Curley couldn't stop the easy smile that lifted the corners of his mouth as he stripped off the tuxedo in the navy ship's bunk. Miss Amanda Chase was more than he'd expected. At first she'd seemed all business, then when he'd picked her up for the dinner and ball she had that knockout gown on that shimmered softly over her curves. Coupled with the innocence in her eyes, it was a dangerous combination.

She apparently didn't know how she affected him. Maybe she merely went about knocking guys out in her own subtle way, taking it all in stride. No, he couldn't believe that. She seemed genuinely taken aback by his kiss. Her sweet surprise wasn't faked. He found that an unusual and intriguing quality.

He began folding the tux to put into his suitcase, when Amanda's earrings tumbled out, sparkling as they bounced off his shoe and under the bunk. He picked them up, almost believing in fate. *Now I know I'll have to return these.* But the first thing on the agenda was to find Eisenburg on a map.

He wrapped the earrings in a handkerchief and put them in his trouser pocket. He closed the suitcase, thinking that he was glad he put the word "postponed" in his note to her. He'd find a way to see her again.

ജ

Amanda cabled her parents when she arrived in London. She exchanged addresses with Ilsa, and said her good-byes in their cabin.

She stayed three days in London. Monday she shopped, buying a rose-colored cashmere sweater for her mother, a gold compact for Victoria, and soft kid gloves for her father, and had the store ship the gifts directly to them. Tuesday and Wednesday she visited her father's gallery and used their typewriter to type some of the ship interviews, and sent two articles to the *Chronicle*.

Helping Mr. Seton, the gallery manager, write a report for her father, she inserted her own note assuring him she was fine, hoping he'd come to terms with her plans. She telegraphed a message to Uncle Jacob that she was leaving for Eisenburg the next day.

Thursday morning Mr. and Mrs. Seton took her to the ferry to Calais. Gazing out over the water, her mind began to drift toward the idyllic evening with Curley. She quickly replaced the thoughts with story ideas. Peering past her reflection in the window, at the water sliding past, she realized she'd have to write a library full of books to cover all the story starts she'd fabricated to stop thinking of him.

Maybe, she thought, *it would be easier not to make such an issue of what was merely a nice evening.* She should simply acknowledge the pleasant thoughts when they cropped up, agree that Curley was an interesting man, shrug her shoulders, and get on with life. She knew, though, it wouldn't work: trying to ignore an evening more fabulous than any other in her life, was futile.

In Calais she boarded a short train to Paris, remembering her school years and thinking that Victoria would have loved being with her. Her Thursday night in Paris was spent quietly in her hotel room, listening to the sounds on the street. The next afternoon she was on a train to Berlin.

Finally out of the city, the lovely eastern France countryside glided by, with cows standing silently on the rolling hills. She closed her eyes, letting the swaying, clacking train gently rock her. The train ground to a stop for a few moments, and when they got rolling again, they passed a mother and her small son carrying their bags into the small depot. Amanda sighed, and looked out at the darkening hills and quaint cottages dotting the landscape.

Now that she realized she couldn't stop evading memories of Curley, they came flooding in, starting with the morning they had stood on the deck talking. She pursed her lips in consternation as she remembered. She considered herself an excellent interviewer, but he had easily deflected her questions. She didn't even have enough notes to fill two column inches.

But she'd had an interesting talk on board ship with an older German gentleman who was returning home. He'd told her that he remembered the terrible times before Adolf Hitler was elected, and that things were so much better now that Hitler had restored order. The wildly inflating money had stabilized, and peace and harmony were everywhere. Amanda sensed his words were too well chosen, sounding too much like they were memorized. When she tried to dig beneath their surface, he angrily cleared his throat, scoffed at exaggerated stories insinuating themselves into frivolous newspapers. He stared off into space, then informed her he had an urgent appointment.

Father, I pray that Uncle Jacob and Aunt Esther are all right. Amanda's eyes flew open as the shrill screech of brakes interrupted her prayer.

"Gelsenkirchen!" the conductor shouted, striding toward the rear of the car. They stopped briefly, then rolled on. She paged through her notebook, scanning the interview for anything of substance. The man was hiding something, but what?

Amanda made herself as comfortable as she could as the train sped through the night. Just after dawn, on the road beside the tracks a group of children waved as they passed. This was the land of Beethoven and Goethe. It looked so peaceful. Maybe the rumors were exaggerated. She'd think positive, and look for the best.

When they reached Berlin at last, Amanda picked up her two suitcases and lugged them through the crowded depot. The noise of hundreds of travelers and the shouts of trains arriving and leaving bounced off the high ceiling, mingling into a cacophonous mush. The warmth of the day lingered in the station, making her uncomfortably hot in her wool coat.

Outside the station, she set the suitcases down for a moment, and took off her coat. She hired a taxi to take her to Eisenburg, and settled in for the ride. She was a child when she last visited Berlin, and this visit was like seeing the city for the first time. The old, narrow streets were clean, people moved quickly, as though they had important business, and Amanda noticed there were no destitute people in front of the well-preserved baroque buildings. She was glad they didn't suffer the same plight as out-of-work Americans dealing with the depression.

The taxi pulled up by the fence in front of Uncle Jacob's house. The driver unloaded her suitcases and she gave him a large tip. The house sat quietly behind its finely manicured lawn and garden. Looking up at the windows, she hoped to see a familiar face.

She pulled her suitcases inside the gate, left her coat draped over them, and walked to the front door. The house echoed the chime of the doorbell, as though a long silence had been broken. She had the odd feeling that something wasn't quite right. The house was too quiet. . .maybe the family was out. . .maybe they were at the train station looking for her. . .maybe—

The door opened and a man frowned out at her. *"Was begehren Sie?"*

Amanda stared at him for a moment. "Who. . .I mean, *Wo ist die Familie?"*

They continued speaking in German. "Where is what family?" asked the man.

"The family who lives here." Amanda glanced around, noting that the house had changed in subtle ways. It was too perfect, like a flawless model. Not like the happy home she remembered where a family lived.

"There is no family here," the man said, and closed the door a few inches, eyeing her suspiciously.

Suddenly the rumors of persecutions came into sickening focus. If they were true, even her appearance at the house was dangerous, both to herself and her family, wherever they were. She forced a slight smile. *"Danke,"* she said, and stepped off the porch.

Back at the gate she put her coat on to dispel the chill she felt. She picked up her suitcases and looked back at the house, feeling that she was being watched. Though she was exhausted, she raised her chin, and set off in the direction of town. Uncle Jacob would be at the gallery, and he'd tell her what was going on.

seven

A breeze flicked Amanda's hair as she walked away from her aunt and uncle's house, wishing she'd asked the taxi to wait. The neighborhood was oddly silent for late afternoon. The houses looked deserted. It hadn't been that way years ago when she, Martha, and Tamara played tag in the front yard.

A small black car slowly approached, its tires snapping a rhythm over the brick road. The two men inside turned their heads, staring at her as they passed. The car glided into the house's driveway. *God, who are they, and what happened to my family?* she asked, turning the corner. The house had lost its friendly glow. She shivered, now thankful for her heavy coat.

Walking and lugging her suitcases made the streets back to town seem much longer. But, she reasoned, if Eisenburg was as large as Berlin she would've had to ask the men at the house to call a taxi.

She recoiled at the thought, telling herself to be reasonable. Maybe they were very nice people, and she interrupted them at a bad time. Maybe they were just naturally grouchy. That sounded most logical. Had Uncle Jacob sold the house to them? Aunt Esther's last letter hadn't mentioned they were moving.

The slanting twilight sun glinted off Eisenburg's baroque buildings. The fragrance of sausage, baked bread, and cooking vegetables wafted past her. She set her suitcases down beside a shop with a large window open to the street. She ordered apple-peel tea and a buttered roll from a thin, mahogany-haired teenage girl who smiled brightly at her.

"Bist du Eng-a-lishe?" she asked.

"Nein," answered Amanda in German. "I'm American."

The girl's eyes widened. She leaned over the wooden counter to peer at Amanda's clothes. "Ahh," she said with admiration.

64

They spoke of American music and fashions. Amanda told her she'd visited Eisenburg when she was very young. She sipped the last of her tea and asked for directions to Drehenstrasse. Pointing and speaking rapidly, the girl told her how to get there. Amanda thanked her and continued on her way.

She walked the three blocks down the main street and half a block down Drehenstrasse, resisting the feeling that something was wrong. An unnatural quiet breathed between the buildings. The gallery was dark, the windows boarded up, and the door had a heavy chain draped across it. A sign stuck inside the bottom of a window said, *"Geschlossen."* Closed.

Amanda stared at the dried leaves blown in and crammed against the bottom of the door. Closed! When had this happened? A slight chill wove its tendrils around her heart.

It was almost dark now. The other stores on the street were closed, and two other stores looked as abandoned as Uncle Jacob's gallery.

Walking away, she noticed someone had scrawled on one of the boarded-up shops the words *"Kauft nicht bei Juden."* Don't buy from Jews?

Two men in uniform walked smartly past her and she hurried to the more lighted main street. The rumors were true! To keep the fears for her family from overtaking her, she concentrated on headlines for her next story. *Jewish Businesses Boycotted in Hitler's Germany, Have Pogroms Really Been Discontinued?*

She sat down on a wooden bench under a dim street light and sighed. It was time to plan her next move. She would not panic, or cause her father to worry until she knew more. *I'm like an actress in a foreign spy movie,* she thought. Her first duty was to find her family.

A few people, strolling after their dinner, passed her. A policeman on the corner fixed her with a bright blue-eyed gaze and approached her. He glanced at her suitcases, then asked if she needed directions.

She gripped the handles of one and started to stand. "No, thank you. I'll be on my way."

He took the suitcase from her. "Allow me, *fraulein*," he said. "Though it's safe to walk our streets after dark, I will accompany you. Where are you staying?" He smiled, waiting for her answer.

Amanda thought quickly. "The main hotel," she said, reaching into her purse. "I have its name here. . . ."

"Come," he said, picking up her other suitcase. "I know the place."

Walking beside him, she wondered briefly if he was the one who boarded up Uncle Jacob's gallery. After they'd gone one block, he turned and led her up the steps into the parlor of a three-story rooming house. He set her bags down and rang a silver bell he picked up from a small table beside the door.

A short, energetic woman appeared and warmly greeted them. She sat at the table, moved the bell, and opened a large registry book. "How long you stay?" she asked with a smile.

"A couple of days." Amanda produced her identification papers and paid the woman while the policeman stood near.

The woman, Frau Reinhardt, led them into the parlor. The policeman left them, pushing the door into the kitchen. Amanda and Frau Reinhardt climbed the stairs to the third floor and walked its carpeted length to the next-to-last room.

Frau Reinhardt adjusted a knob on the radiator beside the door and said, "The bathroom is the third door down the hall, the maid comes to clean at 11:00 A.M., and there will be no visitors, and no music or loud noises after 9:00 P.M."

Amanda nodded, glad she'd had the roll and tea, because her eyes felt heavy, and her head was beginning to pound. Frau Reinhardt left, and Amanda let out the breath she hadn't realized she was holding. She sank onto the faded yellow chenille bedspread, and with her toes pushed off each shoe by its heel.

On a bedside table sat a pitcher and wash basin. A closet door stood open on one wall. Curtains covered a window opposite the door. She was curious to look outside, but too tired to. *In the morning,* she thought, lying back on the cool pillow.

Thoughts of Uncle Jacob and the family dodged in and out of her tired attempts to plan how she was going to find them. She started to doze, but a loud clang startled her as the radiator began heating the room.

She lay there, her eyes closed, adjusting to the noise, letting her mind relax. Curley Cameron's face flashed across her thoughts. His eyes looked deep into hers, a dimpled smile on his handsome face.

She tried to bring her mind back to the problem at hand, but it didn't work. All she could think of was Curley, the sparks, the warm sensations she felt when he kissed her. No man had ever affected her that way. Certainly not Delbert.

The few times Delbert had kissed her, his lips felt cold, and there was no excitement, no thrill. Afterward, her heart continued its steady beating as though nothing had happened. *Delbert's a nice enough fellow,* she thought. *Handsome, rich. But even if I was attracted to him, he still wouldn't be the right man for me, not when he doesn't understand my commitment to Christ. Some girl, though, will be thrilled to be the object of his attention—but not me.*

Curley, on the other hand, had not only thrilled her heart, but he shared her faith. Or had that been just a line? His expertise at kissing was probably all part of a charming act too. Still, he'd seemed so tender when he drew her close and kissed her. She'd never forget the lingering look of wonder he'd had on his face when she finally opened her eyes.

She sat up abruptly, fighting for control. She pursed her lips, telling herself that she was being foolish, falling for a smooth line and a handsome face. *I refuse to think about a man who plays fast and loose with the ladies. Someday I want a man who will offer true love, if there is such a thing.*

Curley must know he'd affected her, since she'd almost shamelessly begged him to kiss her again. *Maybe that's why he didn't show up the next morning,* she decided sadly. These were futile thoughts because she'd probably never see him again.

She'd certainly never be the same naive teenager who'd had a crush on him. She rolled her eyes in relief that she'd stopped short from telling him they'd met before.

Yawning, she got out her pen and paper and recorded today's events in her journal and fell asleep while trying to concentrate on planning a search for her family tomorrow.

❧

That same night while the other guys were celebrating in town, Curley stayed in the barracks. He'd worked hard all week, hoping to finish in nine days and be on a Monday flight to Salzburg.

❧

The next morning Amanda rose early, refreshed from her long sleep. Sometime during the night she'd changed into her nightgown. Now, she opened the window and leaned out into the cool fresh air. Below was a narrow walkway between the rooming house and the building next door. She wondered if Frau Reinhardt tended the row of rosebushes lining the walk.

She shrugged into her robe and took the pitcher to the rest room. A tall, slim woman with circles under her eyes and hair so black it could have only come from a bottle, let her in. "Ach, what a morning!" she said, peering glumly into the mirror over the sink. She pulled the belt of her pink robe tighter around her waist.

"It's going to be a nice day." Amanda smiled at her. The bathroom was as large as her room. Behind a door slightly ajar sat the bathtub.

"You are new tenant?" asked the woman as Amanda washed her hands.

"Yes, I came in last night."

"You speak German with an accent. You are English?"

"No, American," answered Amanda, filling her pitcher with warm water. "Can you tell me where I can send a wire?" she asked.

"At the post office, on the park square. But not on Sunday."

"Thank you," said Amanda. Back in her room, she took a sponge bath standing on her towel in front of the dresser. She put on her gray skirt and orchid sweater and comfortable shoes. Taking her camera and notebook, she left the room.

She followed the fragrance of breakfast to the dining room where several guests were already seated. The long table supported plates of fried potatoes, sausage, eggs, ham, and several other entrees.

Frau Reinhardt, seated at the head of the table, welcomed Amanda, motioning to an empty chair on her left. A red-haired girl carried a pitcher of cream to the table, glancing covertly at Amanda.

Amanda chose a large piece of blueberry coffee cake with streusel topping and poured herself a cup of coffee. The other tenants kept their attention on their breakfasts, hardly noticing her until Frau Reinhardt asked how she liked her room. They nodded in satisfaction when she said it was fine.

The park square was in the middle of Eisenburg, and she easily found the building with "Postamt" chiseled into its exterior. The door was tightly closed and the window shades were drawn, giving the place a forbidding look.

Church bells pealed a somber welcome, and she followed the sound to a gray, ornately baroque building with a few folks climbing the old steps and entering a door that was at least fifteen feet high. The sanctuary was cold, but the majestic organ music was like being at a concert. The service was stately and dignified, with the reading of a whole chapter from Esther which went along with the short sermon.

Afterward, feeling a peaceful calm, Amanda walked away from the church, knowing that since it was Sunday, she'd not make much headway in finding her family. So she strolled around the quaint little town, snapping photos, then went back to the rooming house to write some letters and make notes for future articles.

❧

Monday, Curley was a passenger on a flight into Austria, where he'd pick up a small plane hangared in a field outside of Salzburg. He'd been briefed to enter Germany from the southeast corner, delivering the plane to Holland. His flight would take him over a lot of German territory, giving him a good look at reported growing squadrons of airpower in

Nuremberg, Munich, and Berlin.

Seated in the last seat of the plane, he looked out into the clear black night. The noise of the two engines changed slightly as the plane started its descent. The seven other passengers leaned toward the windows to look down. A row of landing lights glittered in the inky darkness below.

The plane touched down, bounced once, then with a roar slowed and turned around. They taxied to a stop beside a large hangar, and the passengers stood, grabbing suitcases and bundles.

He descended the steps behind the other passengers. Two crewmen stood looking up at the engines. He would have commented that she was a sweet ship, but keeping his anonymity, he didn't. He walked across the tarmac to the barnlike building. Over the door was a sign, *Flughafen von Salzburg*, between tall columns with winged cherubim sitting on them.

Curley followed his fellow passengers across the slate floor, through the terminal. The blond girl and her chaperon were met by a middle-aged man in a gray overcoat. There were no passengers waiting to board the plane he'd just left, and the only people inside were a wireless operator, a clerk, and a stoop-shouldered man pushing a loading cart out the door.

In the chilly night air Curley approached the closest of two taxis. A talkative, gray-haired driver with a large mustache assured Curley he knew the best place in Salzburg to find a room for the night. The clerk in the deserted lobby was so happy to see both him and the driver, Curley was sure they must be relatives.

He signed in, dropped his suitcase in the room, and went to find something to eat. Sitting alone at a linen-covered table waiting for his order, he suddenly wondered what Amanda was doing at that precise moment.

The thought of her made him smile, and he touched his shirt pocket, where he'd stashed her earrings. *I'll be returning these to you soon, Miss Amanda Chase.* He absently stared at the row of mugs on a shelf across the room, thinking of stories he'd heard of persecution and hardships imposed on innocent German citizens. If Amanda asked questions in the wrong places, she could get herself in trouble. He'd find Eisenburg on the map, and fly in as soon as possible.

⋙

The next morning, just after dawn, Curley left the hotel, carrying his suitcase through the streets with their ornate wrought iron signs leaning out over the sidewalks. The graceful old buildings glowed in the early morning light, as he kept the sun behind him. Several signs proudly bore the picture of Mozart, their most famous son.

Curley loped past a blue-domed cathedral and crossed the bridge over a meandering river. The crisp morning air magnified the twitter of waking birds. His steps slowed as he caught sight of a grand old building perched on a hill above groves of trees. It looked as though it had been there for hundreds of years. The dawn light gave the mountain behind it a peach glow, and the oval windows a golden liquid sheen.

At the end of the street a cathedral thrust its ornate spires to the sky, and a group of angels graced the arch over its door, two of them holding slim trumpets between a coat of arms. Curley made a mental note to return and explore this beautiful Salzburg, tucked in the hills of Austria. The cottages became further apart, and soon he was in farm country, with wisps of smoke rising from their chimneys.

He found the airstrip easily, by simply walking west and scanning the vista for a windsock. There it hung on a pole, limp in the quiet morning. He approached the hangar and found its doors open, the Vega's propeller shining in the sunlight.

A tall man, in his thirties, with curly dark hair and blue eyes walked toward Curley. "James Cameron?" he asked, smiling and wiping his hands on a red rag.

Curley nodded, and they shook hands. "Looks like a sweet little bird," he said.

The mechanic beamed, looking fondly at the plane as if he were a mother hen and this was his favorite chick. "You take Vega to Herr Schmidt in Amsterdam, *ja?*"

"That's right." His orders were to deliver the plane within ten days, while observing all he could on the way.

Curley checked it out from tail to nose and found it to be in excellent order. He wasn't surprised, because the hangar was clean and neat. Together they rolled the Vega out onto the grass field, and Curley climbed into the cockpit. Touching his fingers to his forehead in an informal salute, he started the engines.

In the air before 7:30 A.M., he headed northwest toward Munich.

ஐ

That same day, early, Amanda went to the post office in the square. Inside, a row of boxes with numbered brass plates filled one wall, near a counter with a uniformed man standing behind it. Behind him sat a wireless telegraph machine.

She sent a message home, telling them she'd arrived, was fine, and would contact them later. She mentioned that Uncle Jacob and Aunt Esther had moved from their home. Dad might know that the gallery was closed, but until she knew more, Amanda wouldn't worry them unnecessarily.

Outside, in the park, a blond boy in knee britches bounced a ball toward her and she rolled it back to him. She strolled to the other side of the park, thinking. She couldn't simply ask anyone where the family had gone. She couldn't go to the police, because she wasn't sure she could trust them yet.

First she had to see the gallery in the daylight. She turned around and headed in that direction. A young woman in a white apron and nurse's cap pushed a carriage past Amanda. Amanda looked inside the carriage fondly and smiled up at the woman, who stared straight ahead and resolutely pushed the buggy past.

Amanda slowed her steps, pondering the strange impression the town was giving. She'd met a few friendly people, but most of the others went about their business quietly, seeming to shun contact. The cold attitude was conspicuous in the midst of gracious buildings, a charming park squarely in the middle of town, and benches on the main street, made for sitting and chatting. But the people walked through this charming setting with reserved, uncommunicative faces.

The street looked different in the sunlight. On the corner the music store window displayed a gleaming trumpet surrounded by sheet music with the swastika emblazoned on their covers. Amanda walked past a tobacco shop, to the Chase Gallery.

It looked even more forlorn and neglected in the daylight. One of the windows had been broken, and someone had propped a board behind the hole. Scrawled on the board, which she had not seen last night, were the words *Deutshland erwache! Juden verecke.* "Germany awake! Jews perish." A ripple of fear jolted through Amanda. Did anyone take this slogan seriously?

Where had all the artwork gone? She shook her head. Where had her family gone! Backing away, she crossed the street to take a picture of the desecrated gallery.

Further down Drehenstrasse, the other two closed businesses were boarded up, one with a hateful slogan written on its door. She snapped a photo of them also, catching sight of a shopkeeper in his doorway with his hands clasped over his massive belly, watching her. When she caught his eye, he looked away and went back inside.

Something sinister was going on in this town, and a chill crept around Amanda's heart, but she recoiled from it, determined to find the truth. *Oh, God, who can I talk to?* she prayed. *Who's behind this outrage? And where is my family?*

eight

Amanda stared at the door behind which the shopkeeper had just escaped. Four-feet wide, painted gold wire-rimmed spectacles decorated the window, and the man's name was lettered below. She slipped her camera back into its case as she approached.

Inside, she found him concentrating on polishing a black, cylindrical device. Light from the window gilded two mahogany chairs standing before a glass-topped counter.

After a space of silence, he looked up. "May I help you?"

"I'm interested in the art gallery down the street," Amanda answered with a calmness she forced herself to show.

He shrugged and said, "I'm sure there are other art sellers in this town."

"I'd like to know what happened to the people who owned that one." She adjusted the strap over her shoulder to a more comfortable position.

"Why do you ask?"

"I know them, and I'd hoped to see them again." She chose her words carefully, avoiding the Jewish issue.

"They are gone. That's all there is to it." He set the black cylinder down and rubbed the cloth over it one more time.

"Could you tell me where they went?"

He put his hand to his forehead and looked at her reflectively. "You are very persistent about their whereabouts."

Amanda sucked in a deep breath, hoping she was right about him. He didn't seem sinister, just careful. "Mr. and Mrs. Goldstein are my aunt and uncle, and I'd really like to find them."

He stood still for an instant, as if he were frozen, then squinted at her again. He leaned on the counter that separated them, and pulled a card from its depths. "You go talk to Herr

Verendorf, here," he pointed to the name on the card, "he may be able to tell you something."

She took the card and slipped it into her pocket. "Thank you."

"Don't thank me. I didn't tell you anything. And don't tell anyone you talked to me." He moved sideways to look past her out the window. "Now, I think you should go."

She looked over her shoulder but saw no one outside. She thanked him again, and left. Before the door closed, he said softly, "Good luck, fraulein."

❧

Curley navigated the plane through bright blue skies, between snowcapped mountains to Munich, approximately fifty miles from Salzburg. Flying low, he scanned every possible airfield and buildings large enough to be hangars for airplanes. He circled and came back, over the city again, then headed on out to the countryside. Spotting a suitable road, he set up an approach and landed the airplane. He taxied off the road into a field and cut the engines. When he opened the door, the fragrance of harvested wheat rose up from yellow stubble.

He sat there for a few moments, letting time pass. Making too many passes overhead would look suspicious. He reached for his harmonica, then let it slip back inside his pocket. Making music would be redundant in this place.

He took Amanda's earrings from his other pocket. They twinkled in his palm. He pushed them with his finger, making them flash. She had looked so lovely that night on the ship, the earrings sparkling against her creamy skin.

He wasn't the kind of man to put stock in fairy-tale romances, but he'd felt a powerful pull on his soul when he kissed her.

Her green eyes, dark and fathomless, had looked up at him, begging him to kiss her again. *I should have done just that,* he thought. But something had stopped him. Maybe it was her innocent seductiveness combined with open trust. Maybe the intense emotion that hit him and rocked his world upside down just plain scared him.

Before that, when he first landed on the ship, he had felt her standing there, and his eyes were drawn to the one person in the crowd who mattered. There had been instant recognition; that was why he was sure he'd seen her before. He always remembered people he'd met, yet she eluded his memory.

He let out a deep breath, and curled his fingers around the sparkling earrings. The whole event on board ship was probably due more to moonlight, ocean breezes, and a lovely woman in his arms than destiny. He slipped the earrings back into his pocket before his emotions could dispute that conclusion.

He pulled the door shut, admitting that he was looking forward to seeing Amanda again. A few minutes later he circled over Munich once more and spotted an airstrip with large hangars at one end of the field, and several planes lined up near them. He waited while one took off, then when the air space was all clear, he landed.

As soon as he taxied to a stop, two German State soldiers approached him. *"Was machen Sie hier?"*

In his simplified German he answered that he was there to check a noise he'd heard in his engine.

Another soldier approached the two standing beside him. Curley turned to open the plane's door and retrieve his toolbox.

"Halt!"

Curley stopped and slowly turned. The three soldiers glared at him.

"Your papers," they demanded. One moved his hand to the gun holstered at his waist.

Curley grinned. "Sure." He opened the plane's door and reached inside, retrieving his passport. While the soldier studied it, Curley glanced at the facilities surrounding the airstrip.

The soldier grunted, apparently satisfied, and handed the passport back. He told Curley to work on his plane but when finished, to be on his way. To assure that he complied, two left, leaving the third to stand near the plane, watching him.

Unruffled by their distrust, Curley couldn't help wondering if there was something they didn't want him to see. Unlatching the cowling, he glanced at the hangars and planes behind it. He memorized their number and placement.

When he was finished, he put his tools back into the tool-box and hefted it back inside the plane, anchoring it in its place behind the left seat. He grinned at the soldier guarding him and said, "Thanks for the company, sir. I need to use your facilities, then I'll be on my way."

The soldier jerked his head toward the building behind them and led Curley in that direction.

Inside the metal building, thin wooden walls separated rooms, and behind wooden-bordered glass doors was the mess hall. The civilians sitting at tables looked out at them.

"A cup of coffee would sure be nice," said Curley. "Care to join me? I'm buying."

The guard scowled, following him.

"Come now. What harm can I do in the mess hall?" He pushed the door open, and the guard followed him. Curley ordered two coffees and joined a young couple at their table. The guard didn't seem to know if he should stand or sit. Finally, he sat, stiff-backed in a position where he could observe and hear everything at the table.

"Nice day, isn't it?" Curley asked the couple.

"*Ja,* a good day for flying."

"Where are you folks from?"

Their eyes glowed with joy. They glanced at the guard, then the man leaned forward. "From here, but we have just been to Nuremburg to honor our *fuhrer!*"

The woman rolled her eyes. "Such splendor! Thousands cheering, soldiers marching! Four brass bands!" She put her fist over her heart. "Herr Hitler is so wonderful! We cheered his speech for ten minutes!"

Curley nodded and took a sip of coffee. "Sounds like quite a spectacle."

The man beamed. "Our *fuhrer* has unified the people and things are going to be better. You should have seen the girls and boys marching! Germany will soon come into her glori-ous destiny. The future ahead is bright."

"So I've been told," said Curley, smiling. He finished his

coffee and having no further reason to delay, he stood. So did the guard and the young couple. The man said, *"Heil* Hitler!"

The guard hit his chest with his fist. *"Heil* Hitler!"

Back in the plane, Curley took off, craning his head toward the dark planes and large hangars. Two of the doors were opened, and he saw more planes inside. He banked over the buildings, counting eleven large hangars, each capable of housing six airplanes. He counted the planes tied down between the hangars and flew on, northward over the rolling hills.

He circled over Nuremberg, looking for airstrips and more planes, finally landing and inspecting an airstrip as he had in Munich.

He fueled up, left Nuremberg, arcing westward toward Frankfurt, and did the same search, eating a late lunch there. He lifted off, leaving the factories and industrial buildings of Frankfurt behind, and headed northeast toward Berlin. *What a joy to fly,* he thought as the Vega responded smoothly to his handling.

He approached Berlin from the south, looking down at the sprawling city. Three rivers converged, with dozens of bridges crossing them. He followed one river for a while, then circled and criss-crossed over the city, observing three small airstrips. *Somewhere down there,* he thought, *is their glorious leader.* From what his trained eye had seen, Curley knew the *fuhrer* was gathering the beginnings of a powerful air force.

At last he followed a narrow road due east, where the map told him Eisenburg, and Amanda, were. A few miles more and he'd be in Poland, he thought, as he saw the tiny town, seated in a shallow valley. One hill to the south sheltered the hamlet. There was no airstrip, so Curley found the flattest, most remote place he could, and set the plane down. He cut the engines, got out, and pushed the plane behind a bank of bushes.

❧

Amanda stood outside the Verendorf cottage on the hillside south of town. It had taken her two hours to find the place, and her feet were tired. No one answered the door when she lifted and dropped the knocker. She'd gone around to the side of the house, saw a greenhouse in back, but no movement, and no one answered her calls.

Her hand holding Verendorf's card dropped to her side, and she sighed. The nearest house was a quarter of a mile ahead. She slipped the card into her pocket, took her camera out of its case, and started shooting. Satisfied that at least she'd get some good shots of the countryside, she walked up the hill to the next house.

A brown-haired boy with pale blue eyes answered the door. His mother told Amanda that Herr Verendorf had gone to the Nuremburg festival and wouldn't be back for another week. Amanda thanked her, grinned at the child, and walked back to town.

She trudged up the boardinghouse steps, realizing she hadn't taken time for lunch. Tired and hungry, she looked at her watch, glad to note she had a few minutes to rest before dinner.

"Amanda! There you are."

She stopped abruptly at the parlor door and stared. It was Delbert, approaching her with outstretched arms. "Delbert! What are you doing here?"

"Why, darling girl, I've come to rescue you, if you're in trouble, or to help you if you need assistance." He flashed her his dazzling smile.

"How did you know where to find me?"

He gestured to a parlor chair. "Let's not stand here in the doorway. Come sit, and we'll talk."

"I don't want to sit and chat. Please, how did you find me?"

He hesitated for a moment, then said, "Your father called me after you left. He's been unable to contact your uncle, and felt you might need help. So, I dropped everything and here I am."

"I cabled my father I was all right," she said, turning her face away from him. Then, not to be unkind, she laid a hand on his shoulder and said, "Delbert, it was nice of you to come all this way, but I'm taking care of myself just fine. Go back to Boston and tell my father thank you."

"But—"

"I'm tired and I'm going upstairs." She turned from him and walked away.

In her room, she dropped her camera bag on the floor and plopped down on the bed with a long, exhausted sigh. Nothing had gone right. She pressed the heels of her hands over her eyes, to soothe the burning sensation.

How would she find her family? She had no more leads. *They have to be somewhere! If they're in Eisenburg, I'll find them, even if I have to knock on every door and ask everyone in town.* The optometrist might know something more. Even though he seemed nervous about her visit, tomorrow she'd return to talk to him.

She lay back on the pillow and closed her eyes, thinking of her cousins. Were Martha and Tamara in danger? Something sinister was happening. The rumored beatings and tortures suddenly became all too possible. But how could that be in this modern day and age?

She was too tired to think of Delbert, but she appreciated her father's protectiveness. She'd have to keep her doubts and fears to herself. Delbert would approach the situation as a private eye on a federal case. She shuddered, thinking that he could endanger the family, turning their disappearance into an international incident.

At dinner, Delbert charmed Frau Reinhardt and the cook. They piled extra dollops of whipped cream on his dessert, and Amanda hoped they wouldn't credit her for his being there.

The policeman dropped in just in time for the cook to bring him a piece of apple strudel topped with whipped cream. Delbert chatted with him, praising Adolf Hitler for solving Germany's problems, claiming that Americans applauded his efforts to lead Germany into prosperity.

The policeman set down his fork and with shining eyes said, "I was in the crowds at his hotel last summer. There were thousands of us, waving our swastika flags. 'We want our *fuhrer!*' we all shouted. It was splendid." He scanned each face around the table to be sure they were listening. "He stood on the balcony for a moment. Women swooned, but men shouted '*Heil* Hitler!'"

He sat straighter in his chair and in hushed tones added, "The *fuhrer* looked down, and I knew he was looking right at me. Then he spoke." The policeman slowly shook his head. "How wonderful were his words."

The rapt expression on the man's face baffled Amanda. He viewed Hitler as some kind of god. Did Hitler really inspire such devotion? It reminded her of her studies in Roman history. The caesars, proclaimed as gods, brutally eliminated dissenters. *What happened to Hitler's dissenters?* she wondered.

❧

Darkness had settled over the town as Curley walked the road. Behind the western hills the sliver of moon shed weak light over the road, and a chilling wind pulled dry leaves off the trees. Eisenburg was eerily quiet, until a long, black car slid up beside him and stopped. A policeman got out and blocked his way. "Who are you, and where are you going?"

"Jim Cameron. I'm headed for Eisenburg."

The policeman's eyes narrowed as his gaze darted about. "How did you get *here?*"

"What?" Curley bought a few seconds to think quickly. He didn't want to mention the plane, and risk an inspection.

"Herr Cameron, you did not walk from America, *ja?*"

The other policeman got out of the car and stood, listening.

"Oh, no, I had a ride as far as a mile or so back."

"Do you have business in Eisenburg?"

Curley shrugged. "You fellows can tell by my accent that I'm an American. I've always wanted to visit your great country, and now seemed like a good time to do so, since Herr Hitler is bringing such prosperity."

The two officers glanced at each other. Curley hoped these men didn't patrol the countryside, though the plane was well hidden from the road.

The second officer opened the back door of the car. "You come with us. Eisenburg has a curfew, and you cannot be on the streets now."

Curley got into the car, setting his suitcase beside him, and they drove into town. He wondered if they were taking him to jail. But if he'd been in real trouble they would have asked to see his passport.

He looked at his watch. 9:45. The streets were dark, and in the windows of the homes they passed, light filtered through thick curtains with a subtle glow. No one walked the streets, and corner lamps were dimmed.

"Nice town," he said, looking out the window.

He got no response, so he said no more. *God, I hope I'm not under arrest,* he thought, looking out at shops they were passing. *They can't have any idea who I am.* He'd flown over at least two hours earlier. They couldn't know the plane had landed, and even if they had, they couldn't connect him with it. Still, their militant attitude worried him.

When they stopped in front of an official-looking building and roughly pushed him inside, alarm bells began to go off in his brain.

nine

With the disdain of a man who had seen hundreds dragged into the station, a sour-faced guard wrote down Curley's name, took his suitcase, and told him to wait. Curley sat on a high-back oak chair, trying to appear innocent of any violation they could pin on him. Knowing he wasn't didn't help.

There was a gun case full of rifles behind the guard and his desk, and a large painting of Adolf Hitler on the wall beside it. A red flag, with a black swastika within a white circle hung from a pole in the corner.

Curley understood that each nation had its own identity and customs, including flags and pictures of its leaders, but this was somehow different, more aggressive. After withdrawing from the League of Nations, and then in August after the death of President Hindenburg, Germany had overwhelmingly voted Hitler as its *fuhrer*. His promise to bring the people together as "one man" was probably behind the sense Curley had of a clan gathering itself for a confrontation. But with whom? They were just coming out of a depression after a long and bitter war.

Opening a door noisily, the guard who had picked him up and another officer with a bar of ribbons on his brown shirt marched into the room and ordered Curley to stand. They asked him for his passport, asked again what he was doing in Germany, and what his occupation was.

"I'm a mechanic," he said.

A flicker of suspicion glinted in the officer's eyes. "Explain."

Curley lifted one shoulder apologetically. "I do not speak German well, I fix automobiles." That was true; his Tin Lizzie kept him busy. He assured them he was in Germany as a tourist who was interested in the beauty of their land.

"Why are you walking at night into Eisenburg?"

"I explained that. I got a ride to the outskirts of town." The silence lengthened and he stood ramrod stiff, waiting for them to decide he was harmless and let him go. The ticking of a large round clock on the wall pounded like a blacksmith's hammer.

The officer glared at Curley's passport, then thrust it at the guard. "We will keep this until tomorrow. Tonight you sleep at Frau Reinhardt's." He picked up Curley's suitcase, flipped it open, and moved the clothes and shaving kit around.

He snapped it shut and told the guard who had picked up Curley, "Frau Reinhardt has two rooms left. She will not refuse. Take him and tell her nothing." He handed Curley the suitcase.

Curley glanced at his passport on the guard's desk as he walked toward the door. He wasn't sure how good their spy system was, but if it was even mediocre, he could be in hot water very soon.

At Frau Reinhardt's, he stood in his third-floor room, listening to the guard's fading footsteps. The room was at the end of the hall, with a fire escape outside the window. He climbed out and sat on the cold metal, thinking. They knew he wouldn't go anywhere without his passport. But if he didn't get it back soon, he'd have to leave anyway, or face the firing squad as a spy. A light wind rustled the trees behind the building. If it continued, the wind would be a help in getting him and his plane out of here.

How was he going to find Amanda quickly? The town was small, and she was with her family. The police would be no help, but she'd told him her uncle ran one of her father's art galleries. That should narrow the search. He smiled and hunched back against the brick building, thinking of her. In his note he'd said he'd see her soon, but she'd be surprised it was this soon—and in Eisenburg.

The police could become a problem. *I should have waited until I was back in the States and contacted her then.* But he was so near, and he'd felt drawn to her, and. . .

A pebble hit a window about twelve feet away. *A lover's*

tryst, he thought. He hadn't heard footsteps. Slowly leaning forward, moving barely a muscle except his eyes, he squinted down into the darkness below. Another pebble struck the window, then another. The window remained shut. Whoever was being hailed wasn't expecting it.

Then the window opened halfway, and a dark head peered out, looked down, then to both sides. Curley took a quick, sharp breath. Amanda! She looked past him, not seeing him in the darkness. From below came a soft whistle in four quick tones.

He couldn't see the person on the ground, but he heard a "Sh," and then a whispered, "Catch." Amanda held her hands out, and caught something tossed up to her. She grasped it firmly, straining forward and peering down at the person below.

As Curley leaned forward to look down, the metal squeaked. He froze, but Amanda saw him.

⟡

Amanda couldn't believe what she was seeing. Curley Cameron here in Eisenburg, at this very boardinghouse? Impossible! She closed her eyes for a full three seconds, then opened them. He was still there.

He lifted a hand in silent greeting, touches of humor framing his mouth and eyes.

She grasped the rock in her hands so tightly it bit into her palm. She looked down, where her cousin Martha had stood seconds ago, and then she drew back inside her room, completely ignoring the apparition on the fire escape. She couldn't believe he was really there.

Reminding herself that after he'd not shown up at church aboard ship, she'd given up on him, taking him for a fast-talking playboy, she turned on the lamp beside the bed, adjusted the faded silk shade, and then unwrapped the note from the rock Martha had thrown to her. *"Meet me in the park tomorrow at 6:45 A.M. Tell no one, trust no one."*

She put the small piece of paper on the table, smoothing out the wrinkles, reading it again. Why all the mystery? If

Martha was playing a game, it could be fun, but this was no game; the need for secrecy was real.

Amanda folded the note into a tiny square and slipped it behind the mirror in her compact. She turned off the lamp and pressed the round, gold compact between her palms, praying that God would keep her family safe.

She went to the window and looked out. The breeze felt cold against her cheeks. Weak moonlight and shadows gave the walkway below a forlorn appearance. If she hadn't heard the secret whistle she and Martha had shared as children, and had she not held the note in her hand, she'd have thought the whole thing was a dream.

She turned her head slowly to the right. Curley still sat on the fire escape, knees up, forearms resting on them.

"Hello, Princess," he said softly.

"What are you doing here?" she whispered.

"Looking for you."

She stared at him incredulously.

"I told you I'd see you soon. Here I am."

"You're a little late, don't you think?" she said, instantly regretting her petulant tone.

"What?" His grin faded and his eyes probed hers.

"Never mind," she said. "Good night." She started to pull back into the room.

"Wait!" His loud whisper blended with the sound of the breeze. "We haven't finished the interview."

"Good night," she said, ducking back into the room and closing the window.

She climbed under the covers and forced her eyes closed, trying to go to sleep. She reached out and touched the sharp edges of the rock on the bedside table. She said another quick prayer for Martha, Tamara, Aunt Esther, and Uncle Jacob. She frowned. *First Delbert bursts in, just when I don't need him, then Curley shows up.*

She sighed and turned to her side, hugging her pillow. She didn't really care if he was here, she told herself. Why was the first thing she said a rebuke for standing her up at church?

All those years she'd daydreamed of him seemed so silly now that he was here, because the timing was all wrong. Four years ago if he'd appeared in the moonlight, she would have swooned.

She turned to her other side. *I shouldn't let him get to me.* She determined to ignore both Curley and Delbert, and concentrate on finding out what was happening with her family. After all, that and the big story were her mission. *Girl Reporter Shuns Distractions to Follow Story—that's the headline for tomorrow's activities,* she thought.

の

Curley sat where he was for a while, perplexed. Why had she brushed him off? *You're a little late, don't you think?* What did she mean by that? He put his hands into his jacket pocket, fingering her earrings. Who had thrown the item up to her just now? Such stealth was calculated. But why? And why was Amanda here and not with her family? He turned up his collar against the cold wind, pondering these things.

The next morning after a fitful sleep, Curley awoke as the sky turned pale gray. The wind had picked up, and gusts blew the tree limbs, making them scratch against the building. He had a very short time to find answers to his questions, get his passport back, and get back to England with his report.

He was the first person in the bathroom, where he washed up and shaved. Downstairs in the kitchen the cook hadn't arrived yet, so he poured himself a glass of water and took it to the parlor. He switched on the lamp beside a rose-colored brocade couch. A magazine caught his attention. Pages of pictures showed Hitler and his officers at their headquarters with happy people gazing up with awe.

Curley sat and sipped his water, waiting for Amanda to come downstairs. The cook peeked around the doorway and offered him coffee. He eagerly traded his glass of water for it, making her smile.

Other tenants began making their way down to the dining room. Curley joined them for a huge breakfast of sausage, potatoes, rolls, and eggs. He was pouring another cup of coffee when Amanda came in.

He grinned and rose to greet her. The man across from him also stood and said, "Good morning, Honey." Curley composed himself quickly and sat down.

Amanda stood in the doorway, looking from Curley to Delbert. She shook her head slowly and took a seat at the end of the table, between them. She poured herself a cup of coffee and selected a sweet roll.

Curley sipped his coffee while observing the man across from him. *A real dandy,* he thought. His dark hair was slicked back in the latest style, and he wore a striped shirt and a pale blue cardigan sweater. His hands were immaculate, the long fingers lifting the cup almost daintily. His eyes so dark they were almost black, glittered with intelligence. They also seemed drawn like a magnet to Amanda.

She ate her breakfast, conversing in German with the older redheaded woman seated beside her. She didn't look at either Curley or the man across from him. Curley finished his coffee and left. Amanda's glance locked with his as he was on his way out. He nodded. "Miss Chase," he said, and left.

Back in the parlor, he picked up the magazine, waiting for Amanda to finish her breakfast, so he could speak with her alone. He hadn't come all this way just to be brushed off. He'd find out what was going on, deliver her earrings, and get out of Germany. He'd hoped to make a date with her for when they both got back to the States, but she was acting so oddly, he wasn't sure how this meeting was going to turn out.

Suddenly Curley heard two people arguing in low tones. He recognized Amanda's voice saying, "I told you last night I don't need a baby-sitter."

"But, Honey, you know I . . ."

"Don't Honey me! Go back and tell my father. . ." They entered the parlor and saw Curley. She stared at him, then shrugged her shoulders and walked out. Delbert grinned and said to Curley, "Women!" He watched Amanda but didn't move.

Curley did. He walked past Delbert and up the stairs behind

Amanda. He knocked on her door and waited. She didn't answer. He knocked again. "Amanda? Please. I want to talk to you."

The door opened a crack and she said, "I can't talk now. Please go away." He didn't move. She looked at her watch. "Look. I'm busy right now, but we can talk later."

"How about one o'clock in the parlor?"

"One is fine." She shut the door but he didn't hear her walk away. After a moment, he went next door to his room. In less than a minute he heard Amanda's door softly close. He opened his door a half inch and looked out. She was walking away, her camera bag hanging from one shoulder.

She moved quickly down the stairs. He followed her. Outside he saw a man fall into step behind her. The man crossed the street against the wind, still going in the same direction as Amanda.

She stopped at a corner. She looked back, and Curley side-stepped into a doorway. She crossed the street to the park. The man walking on the other side of the street crossed also and turned left. Amanda strolled into the park and seemed to be enjoying the sights. Curley stayed at the corner, knowing she'd spot him if he came any closer.

Amanda sauntered past a girl seated on a bench in the middle of the park. Then she stooped to pick up something, perhaps a rock. The man following her had circled the park and now stood on the opposite side, watching her.

&

Amanda sensed that she shouldn't approach Martha openly, and so she knelt, examining a pebble. "What's happened?" she asked in a low voice. "Have you moved? There were strange people at the house."

"The Nazis took our home and forced us to move into a Jewish neighborhood. They warned us that if we even came near the house we'd be killed."

A shudder coursed through Amanda, and she knew it wasn't because of the cold wind. She stood, brushing off her hand. "I can't believe it!"

"They took the gallery, too."

Amanda walked slowly past Martha. "No!"

"Don't look at me. Ignore me." Martha's pale blond hair was pulled up under a blue scarf tied beneath her chin.

Amanda stood a few feet away, her hands clenched at her side. "Tell me what this is all about." She reached for her camera and focused on a grove of trees and empty swings swaying in the wind.

"Jews are being rounded up into special neighborhoods. Father's business is gone. Tamara had a baby last week, and the circumcision ceremony is tomorrow. If we can find a *moyell* who is willing to come perform it. Everyone is afraid. We've heard awful stories of Jewish people being tortured, cut into pieces, and. . ." Amanda whirled to face her. "Look away. You don't know me!"

"I'm an American citizen, Martha. I came to see you. Where is this. . .special neighborhood?"

"You mustn't!"

"Martha, you know we can trust God to keep us safe. Don't you remember?"

Martha looked at her at last, and said, "It's all so mixed up in my mind. But you look good. I wish. . ." She sighed. "I wish God would help us."

Amanda circled the bench. "Where are you living? I want to come to the *bris*."

"We're at the east end of Domstrasse. Number 22. Tomorrow at nine o'clock. But be careful." Martha stood. Amanda didn't dare do more than glance her way. Martha's gray coat looked like warm armor as she walked with the wind at her back. She wore wool socks and sturdy shoes.

Out of the corner of her eye, Amanda saw a figure approaching from the opposite direction. It looked like one of the men who turned her away from her aunt and uncle's home. She ignored him, focusing her camera on a drinking fountain with a dried-up vine wrapped around it.

Curley watched the man approach the girls and tensed for action. The girl on the bench got up and left. He crossed the street, in case Amanda needed help. She didn't seem to notice the man, and he walked by, looking at her for a moment, then going on. His glance narrowed at Curley as he passed him.

Curley turned and gazed down the sidewalk after the girl in the gray coat. Amanda had hurried to this park, before 7:00 A.M. The only reason could be that she was meeting the girl on the bench. Why? Who was she? The girl was now two blocks ahead. He hurried after her.

ten

Amanda trudged back, the wind pushing her toward Frau Reinhardt's. Something was terribly wrong. Martha's face was pinched and frightened, and her appeal for secrecy alarming.

Inside the boardinghouse, Delbert's happy voice grated on her ears. "You're out early!"

"Yes, I have a lot to do." She smiled weakly at him, trying to be polite.

"You didn't tell how the visit with your relatives went. By the way, I've asked around, and was told there's a baroque cathedral in Eisenburg. We should go see it."

"What?" Thoughts of her family's plight whirling in her brain distracted her from what he was saying.

"I said there's a cathedral we should visit. Bach may have even played there."

Amanda winced. His bright smile was a mockery to the life-and-death situation going on with her family. They weren't in jail, though; or was Domstrasse Street some kind of prison?

Delbert touched her arm. "Amanda? Are you all right?"

"I'm fine. I just have some things to do. Go see the cathedral and tell me all about it later."

"But, honey. . ."

She brought her arm close to her side, away from his touch. His endearment irritated her as much as misspelled words in a headline. "Later, Delbert," she said, heading up the stairs.

In her room she set the camera bag in the closet, beside her suitcase, and splashed water on her face. *First, I'll find a library and read some local newspapers. That may give me a clue to what's happening here. Lord, help me.*

❧

Curley followed the girl in the gray coat. The ends of her

scarf flapped in the wind as she kept her head down against its gusts. Passing a young woman sweeping the sidewalk, she took a wide course around her. The woman shook her broom at the girl and said something Curley could not hear.

The girl hurried on, and Curley passed the young woman who freed the dead leaves from the base of the building to fly off into the wind. She smiled at him. Her light blue eyes were framed by an oval face and shiny blond hair. Nodding politely, he wondered why she showed hostility toward the girl and not to him. He shrugged. Maybe it was some neighborhood conflict.

He followed the girl past a knot of people whom she avoided by crossing the street. Several blocks later the street ended by a barricade across the last few blocks. Guards with rifles slung over their shoulders marched in front of the open gate.

The girl stopped, pulled something from her coat pocket to show the guards, and darted inside.

Curley slowed his steps at the barrier, an ugly fence of rough-hewn brown boards. Both sides of the gate were swung inside. On the fence were signs proclaiming this a Jewish holding area with a Star of David and the word *Juden-Heim* beneath. A white-painted Star of David was scrawled near the signs.

Curley approached the guards. They marched back and forth, their high black boots almost to their knees. A third guard standing beside the gate watched him. He slowed his steps, looking up at the two-story building behind the wall.

"Was machen Sie hier?" One of the marching guards stopped and gestured by lifting his head.

They keep asking me that, thought Curley. *"Ich bin Amerikaner,"* he answered, looking up, as a tourist would, and told them he was just looking. Inside the gates, people were out on the sidewalks, apparently going about their business the same as those outside the gate.

"Hmm." The guard assessed him with skeptical eyes. A third guard came and told the other one to keep moving. He saluted, clicked his heels, and continued pacing before the open gates.

Curley shoved his fists into his pockets, smiled at the blond giant, and nodded at the sign. "What is this, uh *Juden-Heim?*"

The guard took a deep breath, his chest swelling beneath his brown jacket. "This camp is protective custody for our Jewish citizens."

Curley's gaze followed the guards and scanned the fence. "Why do these citizens need protection?"

The man smiled, his blue eyes glittering fiercely. "There are those who look upon them as less than human, worthy only of extermination."

Curley's breath trembled in his throat, and he swallowed quickly. "And you protect them?" This man's feral attitude didn't seem that of a protector.

"We protect them," he snapped.

Curley ran a hand through his hair, smoothing it down in the wind. There wasn't much he could say after that. He took a deep breath, looked up at the rows of barbed wire above the fence. The two guards' boots smacked the sidewalk in front of the gates.

"Well, I guess I'll be getting back to town," he said.

"*Ja,* there are other pleasant sights to enjoy in Eisenburg." He turned and went to stand at his former post beside the in-swung gate.

Curley walked away, looking back once, with the feeling that the gate was more to confine than to protect the Jews from anything outside. What had the young girl done to sentence her to a life in this place? Was she a Jew? How was Amanda involved in this?

He had a lot of questions to answer before he met with Amanda at 1:00. He had a lot to do in a short time.

❧

Amanda slipped out the back door at the end of her hallway and down the back stairs of the fire escape. The wind howled between the buildings, trying to push her back as she made her way to the street. Gray, menacing clouds hung overhead.

She walked a couple of blocks before coming to the bakery where she'd had her first cup of tea. The window was closed against the strong wind, so Amanda went inside.

The mahogany-haired teenage girl smiled brightly when she saw Amanda. "Are you liking your stay in Eisenburg?" she asked.

"I certainly am," said Amanda, inhaling the fragrance of rolls, strudels, and pastries. She chose apple-peel tea and a couple of ginger cookies with thin lemon frosting.

Amanda sat on a high stool at the counter and the girl brought her tea and cookies. "Have you seen the new movie starring Marlene Dietrich?" the girl asked with breathless eagerness.

Amanda sipped the tea and said, "No, I don't get to many movies."

"Oh! I go all the time—that is I wish I could go more. I went to Berlin with a friend, and we stood in line for hours to see Mae West's movie." She rolled her eyes. "All I could see were the wonderful clothes she wore. I wish. . ." A clattering noise from the kitchen area startled her and she snapped her head toward the sound.

"Elisa!" A woman's voice called.

The girl raised her eyebrows and her shoulders. "That's me." She left Amanda and pushed back a gray cotton curtain in the doorway to the kitchen. "I'm coming, Grandmother."

Amanda nibbled on a cookie. She hadn't been able to get a word in edgewise. She'd have to ask somewhere else for what she needed. Thank goodness her tea wasn't boiling hot, so she could sip it quickly. She slipped one cookie into her pocket and drank the last of her tea.

She left some money on the table and was leaving when the girl returned, looking surprised and dismayed. "You're leaving? So soon?"

"I'm afraid so," answered Amanda. "I have business I have to take care of." With her hand on the doorknob she smiled at the girl. "Would you tell me where the library is?"

"Oh, but Eisenburg doesn't have a library," the girl said.

Amanda frowned at the girl's words. "No library?"

"No, but when we need to look up something we go to the school." With pride she added, *"They* have a library!"

Amanda's grip on the doorknob eased, and she asked, "Where is this school?"

"I have to make a delivery, and I go right by there. I'll show you!" She ran back through the curtained doorway and returned, shrugging on her coat while carrying a wicker basket.

They walked down the windswept streets, Elisa chattering away about gowns and hairstyles. They rounded the corner past a church with a steeply sloping roof and decorative ironwork adorning the eaves. "I go to church here," announced Elisa. "Do you go to church? Are you a believer? What town are you from?"

"Yes, I'm a believer, and I go to church," said Amanda. "I'm from a town called Boston."

"Do they have Jews in Boston? My best friend was a Jew, but she's gone to America now. Well, it doesn't matter, I guess." She looked about guiltily and pointed up the street. "That's the school."

"Why do you ask me if there are Jews in Boston?" Amanda looked down into the hazel eyes that looked away quickly.

Elisa shrugged. "I'm not supposed to talk about it." She stopped. A sign over the door advertised an architecture firm. "This is as far as I go," she announced. "Come back soon to the bakery, Miss Boston."

The school, a three-story building, displayed a Nazi flag flapping in the wind on the flagpole. Windows every few feet lined themselves together on each floor. Above the door a huge photo of Hitler in uniform looked down on those who entered.

Inside, her footsteps echoed on the polished wooden floors. She passed a classroom full of children, with books propped in front of them on their wooden desks. On the wall was a picture of Hitler. In the library, racks of newspapers and magazines clustered beneath a portrait of Goethe. She chose several and spread them out on a wooden table.

As she began to read, her heart pounded. She could scarcely

believe the hateful words she was reading. There was nothing subtle about the venom they spewed: Germany was at the mercy of Jews; they were behind every wicked scheme to destroy the country. They were physically repulsive, said one newspaper article; another said they were a lower form of life; "parasites plundering the nation without pity," said Hitler. Joseph Goebbels summed it up: "The Jews are to blame for everything." Cartoons showed ugly, slack-jowled Jews corrupting the morals of Germany; as child molesters, enticing innocent children, seducers of Aryan young maidens, and responsible for every vile sin in the land.

Amanda's stomach knotted up and her blood ran cold. A chill black fog seemed to fill the room. She sat, stunned, for a few moments, with strange, disquieting thoughts racing through her mind. This was too bizarre to be real! Why had none of this made headlines in the States? Rumors and innuendoes were all she'd heard; and they were denied. But they were true! More than that, the rumors were mild, compared to what she was reading.

Uncle Jacob and his family were in danger. She had to get them out of the country somehow. She paged through a few more papers, hoping to find some articles disputing the shocking reports she'd just read, but there were none. She closed the last paper on a drawing describing the unappealing physical and character traits of the Jew.

Amanda looked across the room at the window. It was merely a frame for the dull gray sky. She couldn't shake the feeling of unreality, as if she'd stepped onto the stage of some nightmarish, mad drama. Her fingers moved over the papers and magazines. It was all too real.

A wave of nausea swept over her. She struggled under a heavy darkness that had settled over her mind. Suddenly the door at the end of the room opened, and a teacher led her classroom into the library. Amanda snatched up her purse and fled, willing herself to briskly walk and not run.

Outside, she took several deep breaths, but was unable to calm herself. She walked aimlessly for a long time, thinking, worrying, hoping, planning. No wonder Martha looked so frightened. *I'm an American citizen,* she told herself. *They have no power over me. Or do they?* she wondered. *I am in their country—but still I'm an American.* Having been an American student in France, she knew there were limitations on the power a foreign government had on American visitors, but from what she'd just read, this country's policy was outside all rules of decency and order.

૨૦

At noon, Amanda found herself back at the park where she'd met with Martha that morning. She sat on the same bench, her thoughts churning as fast as the wind shook the trees around her. *I need a plan of action. First, I must find 22 Domstrasse.*

Glad to have some direction at last, she went to the post office, looked at a map of the city, and found Domstrasse. She gasped when she saw the wall drawn on the map. Icy fear twisted around her heart and she began to shake when she thought of the hate she'd read at the library. At one o'clock she pushed the door open at Frau Reinhardt's and started dully for the stairs.

૨૦

Curley was anxiously waiting for Amanda. He heard the door open when she entered, and he saw her walk slowly by the parlor door. "Amanda. In here!" he called. She kept on walking. Something was wrong.

He leaped up and came into the hallway behind her. He touched her arm, and she turned. Her eyes were glazed and full of pain. "Princess! What's wrong?"

She flinched and kept on walking.

Stepping in front of her, he gripped both her arms. "What happened? You can tell me."

She shook her head. "I can't talk now, Curley. I just. . ."

He put his arm around her shoulder. "You look like a girl who could use a shoulder about now."

"I. . ." her voice wavered and she hung her head.

"Come," he said, leading her up the stairs. He opened the door to his room and ushered her in. He sat her on the edge of the bed, and pulled up a straight-backed wooden chair for himself. "Sweetheart, something happened. What was it?"

She licked her lips nervously. "My family. . .they. . ." She remembered Martha's note telling her to tell no one, trust no one. She sucked both lips between her teeth and hugged her arms to her chest. "I can't talk about it."

Curley watched her wretched sadness and understood that she couldn't talk now. In those seconds he was consumed with compassion, wishing he could take the pain and sadness from her.

He knelt before her and gently took her hand. It felt so cold. He covered it with his other hand. "Amanda, I don't want to cause you any more grief, but there are some things I think you should know."

Her eyes had a flat, faraway look in them that alarmed him. "Amanda! Tell me what happened." He looked steadily into her eyes, wishing he could discern her thoughts.

A tear rolled down her cheeks, and he melted. He moved to her side and put his arm around her. "I told you this shoulder is yours if you need it." He drew her head to his chest.

She sat quietly for a moment, then he felt her softly crying. He rubbed her back. "Shh. It's okay. I'm here." He would slay dragons or walk on fire for this woman, he realized with surprise.

He enjoyed her closeness for a few minutes more, until she drew back, sniffling. He reached into his chest pocket and drew out a handkerchief for her.

"I'm sorry," she said, patting the wet front of his shirt.

"It's fine," he assured her. "You needed someone, and I'm glad I was here for you."

"I must look a fright," she said, dabbing at her eyes.

"You look good to me," he said, lifting her chin with his curled index finger. She sniffed once more and turned her head.

"Did you have lunch?" he asked. She shook her head. "I found a quiet little place where we can talk. Let's go."

Amanda paused, as if she was going to refuse him.

"Remember, we have a one o'clock date," he reminded her.

She sighed and said, "I remember."

They sat in a booth of dark wood, in a cozy restaurant. After they'd had a satisfying lunch of dumplings in a dark consomme, they talked small talk, until Amanda began to relax. He asked her what she meant when she'd first seen him on the fire escape. "You said I was a little late?"

Mentioning their date at the ship's church service, she shrugged as if it didn't matter.

"Didn't you get my note?" he asked.

"What note?"

He explained his hasty departure and apologized again. She closed her eyes, enjoying the way his words warmed her heart.

Over dessert, he leaned forward and said, "I told you earlier that I found out some things I think you should know."

Her eyes, like green polished jade, were fixed on him.

"Listen, I notice you're staying at Frau Reinhardt's and not with your relatives."

She opened her mouth to speak.

He held up his hand. "Let me finish." She nodded. "I've been around town, talking to various people, and I have heard some very disturbing things." He leaned forward and lowered his voice. "Hitler has special forces confiscating Jewish homes and businesses, sending Jews into restricted areas."

Amanda winced.

"You know about the wall?" he whispered.

She nodded. He understood now why she was so distressed. She set her spoon down and took a shaky breath.

"I took a look at it," he said. "It was horrible! Like an ugly scar stretching across the street." Curley took hold of her hand and squeezed. "Don't go near that wall. It's dangerous."

"I'll be careful."

"I'm serious. If you have family in there, have them come out to see you. But if you insist on going in, I'll go with you. Do not go there alone."

"How. . ." she clamped her mouth shut.

"How what? How did I find out about your family? That's unimportant for now. What counts is that you need to get away from here. You can work from the States to get your family out."

She shook her head. "You don't understand."

"I understand danger, and this is the real thing. Tell me, are your Jewish relatives believers in Jesus as their Messiah?"

Flexing the fingers of her hand that lay near his, she sighed. "My cousin Martha believed years ago, but I don't think she had the strength to talk openly about it at home."

"Believe me," he said, "the only way to get through something like this is to hang onto God with everything you've got."

Amanda nodded. "That's right. I must get in to see them and pray with them."

"I told you it's dangerous. We can pray together for them. I'm leaving tonight. Come with me."

"I can't do that," she answered, waving his concerns aside.

He admired her valiant determination, but the evil tide he saw building here would engulf her. "You must! There are things here that you don't understand."

"I'm a reporter, remember? I've done some fact-checking on my own, and I understand clearly what's happening here."

The waitress came to clear away their dishes, and they sat back silently, watching.

Amanda opened her purse and pulled out her compact. She flipped it open and turned her head from side to side, patting her hair. She snapped the compact shut and said, "I have to get back now." Her eyes darkened as they fastened on his. "Thanks so much for the shoulder," she said softly.

"Anytime." He stood as she slid out of the booth. He paid the waitress, and reaching into his pocket for change, his fingers brushed against Amanda's earrings.

All the way back to their rooming house he tried to think of a way to tell her of the rumors he'd heard. She may have found out about the German takeover of Jewish businesses and homes, and even of the relocations, but he didn't think she knew that plans were afoot to march Jews out of Eisenburg to some unknown place.

He had been able to glean this information from sources she'd have no access to, by putting together a word here, a gesture there, whispered hints, and fearful constraint which spoke louder than accusations.

Curley stopped outside Frau Reinhardt's. Amanda looked up at him with questions in her eyes. Reaching for her hand, he curled her fingers around the earrings he'd taken from his pocket. "You left these in my care back on board the ship."

Amanda opened her hand and looked at them, then back at Curley.

It seemed perfectly natural to him to lift her hand and kiss the inside of her wrist. "I thought it was a dream," he murmured tenderly. Again, just as on board the ship, he had trouble tearing his gaze away from the moist softness of her mouth.

The door opened, and Delbert looked out, smiling. "Are you all right, Amanda?" He peered at her as she pulled her hand away from Curley. "Did you hurt your hand?"

"I'm fine, Delbert. Just fine." She smiled at them both and swept past Delbert into the rooming house.

You will listen to me, Curley thought, as soon as the door closed. *I'll not leave here without you,* he vowed. He hunched his shoulders against the wind and set out to take care of business. He was, after all, on a military mission.

eleven

Amanda sat on her bed, with her coat on, yet she couldn't stop shivering. The soup she'd eaten hadn't warmed her at all. She slipped off her shoes and tucked her feet beneath her, to warm them. But nothing could warm the icy coldness that gripped her heart.

She needed a plan. But what? Germany had become too dangerous for Uncle Jacob's family. Did they have passports, or were they confiscated? Tomorrow she'd find out at the *bris* ceremony, and she would appeal to the American Embassy if necessary.

She bent the pillow and leaned back on it, pulling the blanket over her. *No one knows I'm related to anyone in Eisenburg—or at least no one except Delbert and Curley—and the optometrist.* Surely, none of them would betray her. Because Uncle Jacob was her mother's brother, their last names were not the same. The ghetto wall crouched at the edge of her thoughts. How could a country single out citizens and segregate them from society? An image of a headline she read today spooled through her memory. *Jews Open A Pandora's Box to Turn Loose Evil in the Land.*

She reached for her pad and pencil. After a moment's thought, she wrote, "Germany's Infamous Secret." Under that she wrote "Millions Suffer Persecution and Humiliation." This was the big story she'd come to find. But she felt no sense of accomplishment. Instead, she felt sick and frightened.

She flung off the cover and swung her legs over the side of the bed. With practiced speed, she wrote everything she'd seen and experienced since her arrival in Berlin, the neatly swept streets, the clean main thoroughfares where tourists walked, and the darker side of the pristine image. She described her uncle's defaced gallery, the ghetto wall. . . She quit writing at last and gazed at the gray ceiling.

The guards! How would she get in tomorrow morning? She could say she was a nurse. But they might demand identification papers. They probably wouldn't allow a tourist in. What if she told them she hated Jews and was glad to see them segregated from the decent people of Eisenburg; would they consider her a sympathizer and let her in? She grimaced at the thought of even pretending to go along with their madness.

There must be a way in, otherwise Martha wouldn't have told her to come. Maybe it was easy to get in, but difficult to get out?

Amanda began pacing the small room, from the window, past the bed, to the door and back. What if she got stuck behind that wall? *I'm an American citizen.* That carried some weight, didn't it? On the other hand, these people seemed callous enough to disregard such courtesy.

She picked up her notebook and sat on the bed again, continuing her notes. Clouds darkened the sky, and afternoon faded into dusk. A knock on the door jarred her, slashing the pencil across the page.

She turned on the lamp and opened the door. Delbert stood in the hallway, smiling down at her. Glancing over her shoulder, he commented, "Working hard, I see."

Amanda glanced back, to see her notebook open and the pencil beside it on the bed. Delbert's handsome face beamed at her. What was he really doing here? she wondered.

She felt better for having recorded her confused thoughts and impressions. Now it was time to deal with Delbert. She sighed. "What time is it?"

He pulled his gold watch from its pocket. "Five-fifteen. May I come in?"

Amanda stepped back and let him in. He sat on the wooden chair, hands on his knees. She stood beside the bed, her hand resting on the table, near the earrings Curley had just returned. "Why are you here, Delbert?"

"I'm glad you asked." Delbert leaned forward. "Maybe I was too bold offering you an engagement ring in front of the family." He flashed her his most brilliant grin. "But I meant it. I do want you to marry me."

"But we already discussed that, and you. . ."

He put up his hand to interrupt her. "I know, I know. I didn't realize how seriously you take your newspaper career. But when you turned me down, and then left the country, I had to face it. I was slightly overbearing." He rubbed his chin slowly.

"Slightly! You called my work 'little newspaper stories.' You absolutely missed the whole point." Apparently her Christianity meant so little, he didn't even think it had any bearing on their relationship. Amanda picked up the earrings and rubbed her thumb across the flat facet of one of the jewels. "Look, Delbert. We don't need to go over this again. You still haven't answered my question. Why are you here?"

"That *is* the point, honey. I see now how important your work is, and I'm here to show that I support you." He gestured toward her notebook. "Are you writing a story about the new government here? Let me help. I can talk to people and get information for you. We can work together!"

Amanda took a deep breath, trying to cover her annoyance.

"Before you say no, listen! While you were out today, I went to that cathedral and talked with some of the local people. The cathedral is magnificent. Bach didn't play there, but Brahms did. And I talked politics to the people. Adolf Hitler has unified the country. He's brought order to the chaos they were in and stabilized their money. Do you know their currency was so worthless, some housewives used it to light fires in their stoves?" He sat back, with a satisfied smile. "Between the two of us we can send back interesting articles to the *Chronicle*."

"Quaint travel articles, telling how lovely it is here, and how happy everyone is?" she asked.

"Exactly. What do you say, honey? Germany, from our point of view! We'd make a good team."

Amanda shook her head. "Thanks for the offer, but I need to do this by myself. And Delbert, please don't call me honey."

He hung his head sadly. "I'm sorry. You asked me before not to call you honey. But it's merely an endearment."

The silence lengthened between them. A thunderclap shook the window, startling her. She looked out, seeing nothing but darkness.

"All right. I won't call you that anymore, but it'll be hard, because you're so sweet." He stood and stepped close to her. Putting his arm around her shoulders, he said, "Please reconsider about working together. We'd make a smashing team."

Amanda moved from under his arm. "Sorry." The room was so small, she had to slip between him and the bed, taking her stance in the center of the room. "So, are you going back home soon?" If she sounded anxious to be rid of him, he seemed not to notice.

"No, I'm going to escort you back when you're ready. Meanwhile I'll be here, helping until then." He crossed his arms over his chest in a self-satisfied gesture.

Amanda clenched her jaw and maintained an even tone. "That's nice of you, but I really don't need an escort."

Delbert raised his eyebrows. "You're aren't at your family's house. Why not?" Raindrops began pelting the window.

She looked away from him, unwilling to go into the story. She put her notebook and pen on the bedside table, then turned to him and said, "I'm famished! It must be dinnertime."

Delbert came forward with his hand outstretched. "I'd take you out to dinner, but it's beginning to rain. However, I'd be happy to escort you to Frau Reinhardt's table."

Amanda nodded. "All right, but I have to freshen up first. I'll see you down there later."

Delbert ran a hand over his slicked-down hair. "Good." His eyes grew serious as he stared down at her.

Amanda stepped back and said, "Later, then." She closed the door, relieved to be rid of him. A headline flew into her mind: *Gullible Delbert Benedict Approves of Nazi Tactics.*

❧

Frau Reinhardt bustled happily around the tables, making sure her guests had plenty to eat. The aroma of meat, potatoes, and vegetables mingled with a spicy cinnamon smell. The good smell, combined with the rain pouring down and beating on the window, gave the room an aura of a cozy island in a cold, blustery world. Amanda and Delbert were seated at one of the smaller tables, set for six. The dining room was full. Most of the residents were there. Minus one. Curley was conspicuously absent.

Had he left without saying good-bye again? She sucked her lips between her teeth. He told her he was leaving, so she shouldn't be surprised or disappointed. *It's just as well,* she thought. She had no time for romantic notions. She had to concentrate on forming a plan to rescue her family from behind that awful wall.

Maybe sometime in the future she'd meet Curley again. He seemed the kind of man who attracted women, enjoyed them for a while, then moved on. A man who might be a good friend, but dangerous to become fond of. She didn't need complications right now. She bowed her head slightly and said a silent prayer of thanks for the food and also prayed for the safety of her family.

Delbert, speaking to the elderly lady with dyed red hair seated across from them, thanked her for recommending a visit to the cathedral. "A magnificent structure," he said.

"Did you also enjoy it?" the woman asked Amanda.

Amanda was on the verge of excusing herself. She had so much to plan and do before tomorrow, and this chitchat seemed irrelevant. "Enjoy? Oh, no, ma'am. I didn't get there. But Delbert told me all about it."

The woman reached out and took Amanda's hand. "There is no substitute for being there. And you can call me Winnie," she said. Wrinkles fanned out from her big brown eyes as she smiled. "Tomorrow will be sunny. I will speak to the priest, and he will open the bell tower for you. Up there you can see for miles. It is a superlative view."

"Thank you. I'll certainly think about it, and let you know."

The woman withdrew her hand with a smile.

Delbert turned to Amanda. "This is a marvelous start to our partnership! Let's do it."

Amanda quickly realized she'd have to leave the house at

dawn in order to avoid Delbert, his questions, and perhaps even an attempt to follow her. Too much depended on her to risk being waylaid by nosey, helpful Delbert. "We'll discuss it later," she said.

Delbert turned back to his dinner with a pleased look.

Between the main course and dessert, Frau Reinhardt checked each table to be sure all was well. She laughed delightedly when Delbert said the meal was as appealing as her sparkling eyes.

She'd just gone back into the kitchen when the front door opened and a cold blast of air whooshed inside. All eyes turned in that direction.

ஐ

Curley brushed the rain out of his eyes and stripped off his soaking jacket. He wished he was wearing his leather flying jacket with the fur-lined collar instead. The warm, fragrant entryway welcomed him.

Frau Reinhardt rushed to him, taking his jacket. "Come, warm your hands in the kitchen," she said, leading him. He walked gingerly, to keep his soggy shoes from squishing. Pausing at the kitchen door, his eyes were drawn across the room to Amanda. For a long moment she looked back at him, then he forced himself to turn and enter the kitchen.

Steam enveloped him with another warm welcome. Frau Reinhardt spread his jacket over three wooden hooks near the back door and placed a towel beneath to catch the drips. The cook moved a pot from one of the burners, and Curley warmed his hands. "This is just what I needed. Thank you." He grinned at Frau Reinhardt.

"A night good only for ducks and fish," observed Frau Reinhardt.

Curley rubbed his hands briskly. Though they were warming, his feet still felt frozen.

As if Frau Reinhardt read his mind, she said, "You have dry socks in your room, *ja?*" He nodded. "Go on, then. Warm your feet. Your dinner will be on the table when you come back down."

He touched his forehead in a mock salute. "Aye, aye, captain."

Back in his room Curley turned on the radiator and removed his shoes and wet socks. He tied his shoes together with the strings, removed the picture over the radiator, and hung them on its nail. The radiator clanked and ticked as it began heating. He draped a sock to hang from inside each shoe. A drop of water fell on the radiator with a hiss.

He removed his passport from his shirt pocket. The police had given it back with strict orders that he be gone by tomorrow noon. He'd strolled past the edge of town, then jogged out into the country to check on the plane. He found it just as he'd left it. He thanked God for the high winds and threat of rain that kept curious country folk inside.

It wouldn't be smart to take off in the storm, though this sweet little plane could do it, and Curley had the expertise to fly out, if necessary. Early would be the best time to leave, and if the storm eased up and the westerly wind continued, he'd make good time.

Back in the dining room, Frau Reinholdt directed him to sit next to the redheaded lady across from Delbert and Amanda. "You sit with your American friends. Relax."

He inclined his head to Amanda, Delbert, and the lady beside him. Giving quick thanks for the meal set before him, he felt a strange comfort at being so near Amanda.

She and Delbert had finished eating and had coffee cups at their places. Delbert laughed at something Winnie said. Amanda sipped her coffee, gazing distractedly into her cup. Long lashes lay against her cheeks. Curley flexed his fingers, longing to lift her chin and look into her clear, observant eyes.

Just as if he'd done so, she looked up with a burning, faraway look. He tilted his head and leaned forward. "Hello?" She focused her eyes, startling him with their soft emerald glow.

Delbert looked from Curley to Amanda. He laid his hand over hers, and Curley didn't miss the implication of possessiveness.

Amanda slid her hand out from under Delbert's and stood, excusing herself, and Curley and Delbert rose. Curley thought, *I have to talk to her alone and warn her of the danger out there.*

Back in her room, Amanda began her preparations. She wrote a letter to her parents, sealing it in two envelopes so that it would be difficult to hide any tampering.

She tapped her pencil on her chin, contemplating her next step, when her eyes caught sight of a small piece of paper lying on the worn burgundy linoleum just a few inches inside the door. It hadn't been there when she went down to dinner, and she must have pushed it aside when she'd come in just now.

She quickly unfolded it. Inside was a small yellow triangular patch. "Pin this, point up, on your chest, left side," was written on the paper, signed "M."

A chill zinged up her neck and her gaze darted about the room. How did Martha get this message here? All day Amanda had wondered how Martha had known she was here, and now this.

The rain beat against the window, sliding down in watery rivulets. She fingered the patch, looking toward the rain-streaked window, trying to remember details she'd read at the library. Certain citizens were given a serial number and triangle. Red for politicals, green for criminals, purple and black for something she couldn't recall, pink for homosexuals, yellow for Jews. Holding the actual symbol made it all more terribly real.

A knock at the door startled her. She crammed the note and yellow triangle into her pocket and opened it.

❧

Knocking on Amanda's door, Curley reminded himself to be patient. As a captain in the air corps, when he issued an order it was obeyed without question. He wasn't used to the art of persuasion. But persuade her he must.

The door opened slowly, and Amanda stood in a soft dark pink sweater and slim skirt, with the glow of the lamp behind her. She looked feminine and vulnerable, and he relaxed.

Convincing her might not be as hard as he'd thought.

"Curley! Well, this is a surprise." She glanced at his stockinged feet. "You didn't even wait for your shoes to dry." She stepped back. "Come on in."

He entered, leaving the door slightly ajar behind him. The only evidence of her occupying the room was the tablet on her bed and a wet washcloth draped over the radiator pipe.

"Did you come to say good-bye?" she asked.

He leaned his shoulder against the door and crossed his ankles. "Yes. And I'm asking you once again to come with me."

She raised an eyebrow. "And why should I do that?"

He pushed himself away from the door and stood with his legs apart. "I told you, the situation here is much more dangerous than you realize."

"Thank you for your concern, but I *am* an American citizen, and an observer, and I'm not going to do anything to draw attention to myself," she answered in a determined tone of voice.

He reached out and gripped her arms. She looked up at him with wide, surprised eyes. "American citizen or not, you'll be in danger if you stay," he said, more harshly than he intended.

She frowned, her eyes darkening. "I saw. I read the hideous lies and actions against certain citizens. But I see no danger to me."

Curley realized his hold on her was tightening. He let go of her arm. "Listen, and don't ask me how I know, but soon, maybe tomorrow, the police will take a group of its 'protected' citizens from behind the wall, to some unknown place."

Amanda's mouth tightened a fraction. "Which group?" She reached for her tablet and pencil. He reached for her wrist.

"This is not to be written, yet. I don't know which group, but they will be Jews." Her raised chin of defiance irritated him. "Amanda, I'm telling you—leave now."

She looked away, not answering. Her wrist felt birdlike and fragile in his large hand. He moved his thumb and marveled at the velvet softness of her skin. He let go of her and she seemed to relax.

Gently rubbing her wrist, she said, "I can't leave right now, but I do thank you for the warning. I'll be careful."

He stared at her, wanting to shake sense into her, to tell her of the brutal look in the eyes of the guard at the wall. He couldn't explain the vicious ways of fighting men. She knew nothing of such things. "We need to pray," he said, unable to keep quiet. "Now." He reached for her hands.

She looked startled, but obediently she bowed her head.

"Father God," he began, "You have power over every evil in the world. I pray now for Amanda's safety, and for her family's, and. . ."

When he finished, he let go of her hands. "If you change your mind, you know where my room is. I'm leaving at dawn." He did have his orders to report soon.

She followed him to the door. "Thanks. And good-bye."

Curley gave in to the impulse to touch her shoulder. The lamp behind her again surrounded her in a soft glow picked up by the sweater's fine wool. "I want to see you after we both get back. Will you give me your address and phone number?" He could feel the magnetism that pulled him when he was close to her.

"All right," she said almost in a whisper. Her gaze dropped from his, and she moved away to pick up her tablet and pencil. She wrote on the bottom corner of the page and tore it out. Handing it to him, she smiled and said, "Well, then, this is it. Good-bye, and Godspeed."

This isn't a final good-bye, he thought. He'd see her again. He'd walk through hell and high water if he had to.

An overwhelming need to hold her swept over him and he drew her to him. He held her in his arms for a long moment, simply enjoying the feel of her softness against him. She brought her arms around his waist and sighed. He dipped his head and kissed her cheek, her chin, then settled his mouth on her lips.

She raised herself on tiptoes and moved her arms to his chest, then slid them up around his neck. The warmth of her lips ignited a fire that flared through him. He pulled back briefly, then reclaimed her lips again. The delicious joy that resulted almost drugged his senses. He pulled back, and crushed her to his chest.

He rocked back and forth a moment, then kissed her on the forehead. "May God take care of you." He looked into her eyes which were smoldering with embers of desire.

"You too," she whispered. Before he gave in to his urge to stay there and kiss her all night, he reached behind him for the door knob. She slid her hands from his neck and clasped them at her waist as he left.

Back in his room Curley sat on his bed running his fingers through his hair. He had his orders to get that Vega to Holland. Of course, they'd given him plenty of time, but he'd already delayed his takeoff until tomorrow at dawn, hoping to take Amanda with him.

He remembered when his best friend Johnny met Meredith. Curley was only fifteen at the time, but he'd thought Johnny was foolish, even though Meredith was a special woman. Just last spring Johnny had told him that someday he'd find a woman who could inspire him to walk through fire or flood for her, just as Meredith had inspired him. Curley had scoffed then.

Now he began to see that until Amanda came into his life, he'd led a lonely, single existence. It was as though he moved all alone among people who connected with each other, never allowing himself to think there was anything missing in his own life.

He placed his elbows on his knees, hands clasped behind his neck, remembering back ten years. When Meredith came into Johnny's life Curley was sure that such a perfect match was something that only happened once every century.

Lately, though, he was beginning to feel the stir of something in the corner of his heart that had been locked away from the time he was four years old when his mother left. Amanda seemed to be able to reach past his defenses and touch the childlike hunger for love and acceptance.

Curley covered his face with both hands. Since Amanda came into his life, nothing was the same—that thought alarmed him more than he wanted to admit. He took a deep breath and went to the closet for his suitcase. He had a mission, and the sooner he got his mind on that, the better off he'd be.

He packed everything, closed the suitcase, then lay on the bed, fully dressed. "God, take care of her. She doesn't know the danger she's in. But You do." He closed his eyes, drifting in and out of sleep until dawn's thin light crept into the room.

twelve

After Curley left her room, Amanda leaned against the door for support. She had dreamed of being held in his arms, but his unexpected gentleness awakened a deep feeling of peace in her heart. She took a ragged breath, surprised at her swift and passionate reaction to him. She stroked her arm, conscious of the lingering feel of his arms holding her close to his warmth.

She touched her lower lip, still warm from his kiss, inspiring an intense desire for more. She forced herself to walk across the room, away from the door, afraid of her need to go after him. She stood watching rain streak the window, and she jammed her fists into her sweater pockets.

The yellow triangle bristled against her right knuckle, as if an iceberg were thrusting itself up through her warm sensuous haze. She retrieved the note and angrily tore it to shreds. She opened the window a crack and let the storm grab the pieces.

She pushed back the closet curtain. Moving the clothes about, she finally pulled out a classic navy blue skirt, matching jacket, and white blouse. From her purse she got two safety pins and pinned the triangle to her overcoat lapel.

She longed for someone to confide in, but there was no one. Even Curley, who saw the danger, wouldn't understand her need to stay and help. She almost wished her father were here. She knew, however, that even if he were in the next room, she couldn't tell him. He'd tell her to stay in her room, then he'd take over and demand the release of his family.

But would that be the right thing to do? No. She'd done her research at the library, and she was well aware that this persecution ran deep. To face it head-on would only result in being crushed.

She stared down at her camera bag on the floor. She would take pictures of her new cousin and the rest of her family at the *bris,* but getting the camera past the guards would be tricky. She unlatched the flash attachment, took it apart, and laid the pieces, along with two new rolls of film, on the dresser. She slid her notebook inside her purse, glad now that she hadn't surrendered to the fashion rage for pert little clutches.

After washing her face and brushing her teeth, she put on her pajamas and climbed in between cold sheets. Hoping for a little sleep before dawn, she tried to push Curley and the Nazi problem from her mind. The tip-tap of the rain and the metallic noise of the radiator lulled her to sleep.

She woke with a start. The rain had eased, and the silence was heavy. She bit her lip, hoping she hadn't cried out. She'd been dreaming; she was in a large garden, fleeing from a menacing pursuer. She came to a pond, and tried to go around it, but it grew to become an ocean. Waves crashed at her right, and her pursuer was closing to her left. She saw a bridge ahead and ran faster, but her legs felt as if they were running through glue.

Uncle Jacob, Aunt Esther, and the family were on the bridge, looking out to sea, unaware of her plight. She shouted a warning, but they smiled, waving at someone in the distance. She glanced over to see what the family was waving at. It was Curley, falling into the water from the sky. *No!*

Her heart was still pounding. She flicked on the lamp and looked at her watch. Three-thirty. She turned the lamp off, and lay back on her pillow, wondering who was chasing her in her dream. What was her family doing there? She trembled at the vision of Curley falling from the sky. The sky was his milieu. She'd seen him perform breathtaking stunts when he was a teenager. He'd parachuted flawlessly onto the ship just two weeks ago. So why did she dream of him falling?

She understood the part about her family on a bridge, unaware of the peril; but the peril was theirs, not hers. She thanked God that He'd promised to walk with her, even through the valley of the shadow of death. *Lord, help me to speak up tomorrow, so they'll know they can trust You, no matter what the circumstances. Please provide an opportunity o show them the Gospel.*

She turned to her side, puffed the pillow, and forced herself o relax, knowing she'd need to be alert tomorrow. Actually n just a few hours.

She drifted on the edge of sleep, and when the night light-ened to pewter gray, she sat up and put her feet onto the area ug beside her bed, adjusting to the semidarkness.

She wrapped her robe around her and hurried to the bath-oom. Then she heard a noise. Holding a damp washcloth in ne hand, she opened the bathroom door with the other, then roze. The weak light showed Curley standing beside her bed-oom door. With suitcase in hand, he paused there for a noment, as though listening, or making up his mind about something. Then he scowled and strode down the hall. She quietly pulled the door shut until he'd gone past and had plenty of time to get down the stairs.

Back in her room she brushed her hair until it crackled, hen gathered it in a clip at her neck. She finished dressing and slipped the flash attachment parts into her jacket pock-ets. Opening her blouse, she slipped in the camera, settling it uncomfortably above her waist. Over all of this she wore her overcoat.

She stole quietly through the house and slipped through the front door into the frigid morning. The sky had lightened to a silvery color. Breathing in the fresh scent of rainwashed pave-ment and wet bricks, she put on her scarf and gloves. The air chilled her cheeks. She checked her watch: five fifty-five.

At the corner she turned left for a few blocks, then pro-ceeded down a street that parallelled Domstrasse, toward the barrier. As she got closer she detoured another block, to Eisenburg's last street, in order to approach the wall as far from the guards as possible.

A block to her left was the wall's corner. She went around the corner, determined to walk all around the confine. How big was the walled-in area?

To her left were rows of fruit trees with their branches stripped by the wind. Amanda walked the path beside the

wall for approximately five city blocks, tiptoeing in som
places to keep her heels from sinking into the moist earth.

Wisps of smoke rose from behind the wall and she coul
hear doors opening and the faraway murmur of voices. Sh
thought she heard someone behind her and looked aroun
quickly, but all she saw was an orange cat darting into th
orchard. She folded her coat lapel with its yellow triangle t
the inside and kept walking.

She followed the encircling wall to the front which face
Domstrasse. She checked her watch again: six forty-five. Sh
passed the only gate, and walked on a few blocks down nar
row streets, passing somber, unsmiling people.

How would they react if she turned her lapel out and the
saw the yellow triangle? She didn't, reluctant to risk the stin
of discrimination toward Jews. Was this in a small measur
what her family lived with? The thought, even for a few min
utes, was offensive, but how did a person live with it daily?

The aroma of coffee and sweets baking distracted an
tempted her, but she didn't think her stomach could handl
food. A middle-aged man seated at a table near the baker
window looked up from his newspaper and gave Amanda a
appreciative glance, with a warm, friendly smile.

He looks like a nice person, she thought. Would he smile i
she turned her lapel outward to show the yellow triangle
What would he say if she interviewed him about his country'
policies toward Jews and other "inferior" groups? It was har
to believe that these seemingly normal, nice people woul
support such repulsive decrees.

The bakery door opened and someone came out. That'
when she saw the sign, "No Jews Allowed." Her stomac
knotted up and she turned back the way she'd come. *I'v
avoided this long enough,* she thought, pulling her lapel out t
expose the yellow triangle. She was a fool to tell herself sh
was merely gathering information, learning more about th
town, when the truth was she delaying going inside tha
hideous fence.

She took a deep breath, held her head high, approaching th

gate where a guard stood at each side. She looked straight ahead and walked inside.

"Halt!"

Pushing back a surge of anxiety, she stopped. She took another quick breath and looked back. *"Ja bitte?"*

"Where have you been?" His eyes narrowed.

"On an errand," she answered as calmly as she could.

"I'd remember you," said the other guard with raised eyebrows. "You did not leave this morning."

Amanda looked him straight in the eye. "Maybe you were in the gatehouse."

The other guard adjusted the gun strap over his shoulder, eyeing her. At that moment a truck full of soldiers roared up to the gate, distracting him. His gray eyes hardened at Amanda and he sneered, "Move on, Jewish whore!"

Amanda felt her cheeks burn as she turned and hurried inside. Her legs weak, she steeled herself to keep going and not look back. As she gritted her teeth, trying not to reveal her anger, she began noticing details. The street and buildings didn't look so different on this side of the wall, but there was a sense of despair in the few people who shuffled passed her. The light of hope gone from their eyes, they didn't speak to each other. Her footsteps echoed loudly in the quiet street.

An old man with a beard down his chest gave her a skeptical look, then he crossed the street as if to avoid her. A baby's cry from overhead pierced the silence. Amanda glanced up. The dark second-story windows all looked the same. She moved on, staying close to the building so she'd be less visible to the guard in case he was still watching her.

She turned a corner and continued walking the oddly silent but occupied streets. She encountered no guards. Apparently they didn't enter the confine; they simply guarded the gate.

She stopped at a stone wall, took out her notebook and pen, and jotted some notes. Her anger stirred as she wondered why there was no outrage, no reports of this monstrous assault on whole segments of a country's citizens.

That anger energized her as she went back to Domstrasse

and found number 22. Carved figures sat upon ledges over the doors, and wrought iron railings enclosed minuscule garden spaces, most filled with yellowing grass.

By now it was almost 9:00, so she mounted the steps and opened the door. Her eyes took a moment to adjust to the dark foyer. She stood in the dim hallway, confused for a minute, wondering how she'd find the right door. The foyer smelled of old wood, lemon oil, and mint.

She was searching for a list of the occupant's names, when the door behind her opened. Her cousin Tamara, with a blanket-wrapped bundle in her arms, entered with a man. They squinted at the darkness.

"Tamara!" Amanda touched her cousin's shoulder. "It's me, Amanda."

"Amanda! I'm so glad you've come. But it's not safe."

"So everyone keeps telling me." She nodded at the man with Tamara. "You must be Nathan. I'm glad to meet you."

A door opened behind Nathan, and Tamara nodded at the old woman who looked out. "Hello, Mrs. Mandelbaun." The woman looked uneasily toward Amanda and shut her door without a word.

"Come on." Nathan motioned, leading them behind the stairs.

The door opened into a short hallway so narrow they had to walk single file into the tiny studio apartment. The room had one small window looking out onto another building.

Uncle Jacob approached them with hands outstretched. *"Mazeltov!* Enter! Enter!" He embraced Tamara, then gave Amanda a glowing smile and hugged her too.

Amanda, so glad to see her uncle, tried to ignore the shock at seeing the family reduced to living in such cramped and shabby quarters. She hugged him back, and he kissed her on both cheeks.

Smiling broadly, Aunt Esther entered from the kitchen with a wooden spoon in her hand and Martha right on her heels.

"Amanda!" Martha anxiously waited for Aunt Esther to step back from hugging Amanda so she could hug her long and hard. She stepped back with a confused look. "What's this?" She felt the bulge at Amanda's waistline.

Amanda laughed. "My camera. I smuggled it in."

"It's good to see you still have your sense of humor. We're so glad to see you," said Aunt Esther, and added sadly, "but not in these circumstances."

Aunt Esther took Amanda's coat and said, "Have you seen our little David?"

Tamara had unwrapped the blanket and smoothed back the baby's dark hair so they could admire his ruddy-cheeked face. She looked up at her mother with a worried frown. "Are Rabbi Benjamin and the *moyell* coming?"

"They said they would."

Nathan shrugged. "They are afraid." The defeated words fell heavily into the silence.

Uncle Jacob waved toward the small sofa. "Sit and tell us what's happening in America. We don't get much news here."

Amanda sat, close enough to the edge to leave room for Martha. "Dad and Mom are doing fine. Business is good, since most of our investments are in foreign countries. You've probably heard there's a depression in America. But President Roosevelt has everything in hand. He's instituted programs to keep people busy earning a little money."

Aunt Esther called through the kitchen arch, "Talk loudly, so I can hear!"

"This place is so small, you'll hear us breathing," said Martha. She squeezed Amanda's hand and whispered, "There's so much I want to tell you."

Tamara and Uncle Jacob sat on wooden chairs, while Nathan stood behind Tamara, his hand on her shoulder. Amanda glanced around while she assembled her camera, wondering where they slept. There was the room they were in, a cramped kitchen, and probably a closet behind the fringed material hanging over a shallow doorway.

She didn't want to cause her uncle sadness, but she had to ask, "What happened to the house? I went there, and found some very unfriendly men."

Uncle Jacob's eyes blazed. "Those. . ." he fumbled for a word, "those poor excuses for human beings, they ordered us out of our own home."

Amanda stared at him, dumbfounded. "By what authority. . . how could they do that?"

"Just walked in and took over." Aunt Esther stood in the kitchen doorway, fists on her hips. "We had to scramble to gather together what we could carry out." Her accusing voice grew sharp. "Those worthless curs have our family china. They better not eat off it!" The thought of that seemed to incense her more, and she added. "I'll have to disinfect everything."

Amanda liked her aunt's feisty expression, and she took her picture. She lowered her camera. "You're going back? When?"

Uncle Jacob stroked his chin thoughtfully. "I expect we'll be back home before Hanukkah." The whistling teakettle got Aunt Esther's attention and she went back into the kitchen.

"Then you believe this displacement is temporary?" Amanda took a candid pose of Tamara, Nathan, and the baby.

"Most certainly," said Uncle Jacob. "It's a passing thing. The Nazi party wants to show its strength, that's all. This will all blow over in a month at the most."

Amanda thought of the newspapers she'd read yesterday afternoon. "The gallery. . ."

Uncle Jacob's face blanched, his fists clenched. Aunt Esther saved the tense moment by entering the room, asking Amanda if she wanted her tea with sugar and apologizing that they had no cream.

There was a light tap on the door and Martha jumped up to answer. She ushered in a stout man wearing a heavy black coat, and a *yarmulke* on his head. He carried a small case in his hand and had the friendliest eyes Amanda had seen since she entered Germany.

Uncle Jacob and Nathan greeted him and clasped his hand. "Rebbe Stein. Welcome."

"Rebbe Benjamin sends his prayers for your family."

Uncle Jacob introduced him as the *moyell,* and Aunt Esther offered him a tray of scallop-shaped cookies pressed together with jam inside and powdered sugar sprinkled on top.

He took one, thanking her, and she handed him his tea. He sipped it, and touched the baby in Tamara's arms, saying, "We must wake the little man and hurry with the ceremony. I am sorry, but I feel there is trouble brewing outside."

Amanda shuddered, remembering the nastiness of the guard and the soldiers arriving as she entered the gates. She shot a picture of all of them, the baby in their midst.

Tamara prepared David while Rabbi Stein opened his black case. He said the ceremonial words, then circumcised the child, who began wailing.

Tamara hugged the crying baby to her breast, while Nathan thanked the rabbi.

He washed his hands, using a special cloth he'd brought, and repacked his case. He took a quick sip of tea, picked up a cookie, and apologized for having to leave so abruptly.

Tamara handed the baby to Aunt Esther and followed Nathan as he walked Rabbi Stein to the door. "We understand. Thank you," said Nathan, seeing him out.

Aunt Esther cooed softly to the baby and he stopped sobbing. Amanda picked up her teacup and asked Martha, "How did you know I was at Frau Reinhardt's?"

Martha smiled. "It was—"

Gunshots suddenly stabbed the air, popping over and over. Panic swept through Amanda. She set down her teacup with shaky hands. Aunt Esther's eyes widened in fear. The baby wailed again, and Tamara cried, "Oh God, help us!"

The warm family gathering was shattered by a bullhorn. A roaring voice yelled, "Everyone out! Anyone left in this building in two minutes will be shot! Out! Now!"

thirteen

Amanda gaped at the furious activity. Aunt Esther scooped something golden and twinkling from a jar on her cupboard shelf; Uncle Jacob, with knees bent, reached deep into the closet; Nathan stood clutching the bawling baby while Tamara, with tears streaming down her face, stuffed his new booties and sweater into the diaper bag. Martha had her hands in an open box, pulling out warm woolen scarves, socks, and hats. Then she reached beneath the couch to retrieve a small notebook and pen.

It all happened so fast, Amanda stood as if in a dream, watching. Martha bundled the warm woolen items into a scarf and tossed Amanda's coat to her. "Hurry!"

Amanda woke from her shocked daze. She shrugged her coat on and quickly unscrewed the flash attachment from her camera, then stuffed all the pieces into her pockets. "What can I do? Can I carry something?" She looked about helplessly.

"You're an American!" shrieked Tamara wildly, thrusting her baby into Amanda's arms. "Say he's yours. Take him to America. He has no chance here!"

Amanda shook her head, startled and shaken. "But I. . ."

Nathan reached for his son, and put an arm around his distraught wife. "This is temporary. We'll all go home when—"

"Come!" Uncle Jacob held the door open while they filed out. Martha carried the bundled scarf in one hand and took Amanda's hand with the other when they got out into the dark hallway. Footsteps hurried down the steps from the upper floor. The woman in the front apartment walked unsteadily out the front door, clutching a shawl to her neck. Tamara's baby had grown quiet and the silence was broken only by the sniffling of a young boy holding his mother's hand as they walked out into the dim sunshine of an unknown future.

On the front steps of the building, Amanda could barely believe what she saw. German soldiers stood with rifles pointed menacingly. Some used them as prods to move people huddling in the middle of the street. It reminded her of pictures she'd seen of cattle drives. People were being rounded up in the street!

Those emerging from the building behind her streamed around her. "Come on!" urged Martha, "before they use force on us."

A soldier approached, glowering, and Amanda followed Martha into the street, to stand with her family. Fear and confusion threatened to erupt into hysteria as people looked from one to another for an explanation, a shred of hope or dignity, and found none.

All I have to do is show my passport, thought Amanda. She decided to wait, to endure what lay ahead with her family. Maybe the soldiers assembled the people to give new rules, or to frighten them by a show of strength. Amanda put an arm around Martha. Nathan had an arm around Tamara, supporting her while she cried softly.

Uncle Jacob turned his head from side to side, as though looking for a logical reason for this ousting of people from their temporary homes. Aunt Esther glared at the guard stomping through the crowd. Amanda had seen that look before, when she and Martha were children and had gotten into trouble. They always said that look could make a stone tremble. *These soldiers are harder than stone,* thought Amanda. *They won't tremble; they'll strike back.*

Amanda reached out to touch Aunt Esther, when all of a sudden they heard a wail from the building across the street. A soldier emerged from the doorway, behind an old man who was clutching his hip and limping. *"Schnell!"* shouted the soldier and whacked the man across his shoulders, sending him sprawling down the steps.

Reacting quickly, Amanda dashed to the old man's side and helped him to his feet.

"Leave him!" snarled the soldier.

Amanda looked up and muttered, "He's hurt."

The icy gray eyes filled with contempt, sending a chill down her spine. "Vermin have no feelings."

She bit back an angry retort as the old man struggled to his feet.

The soldiers began pushing and urging the crowd to the gate. Faces near her looked about in panic. There were no explanations, only shouts and prodding. No one dared question the soldiers, but a raw, primitive dread shot through the group.

A suffocating tension gripped Amanda's throat. She grimly noted every nuance and action. *Outrage in Eisenburg* would be her next headline.

Curley had warned her of this. She suddenly longed for his strength. She looked up; was he up there in the skies, gone from this madness? And Delbert. What would he do? He hadn't been able to sense any trouble was brewing. Visiting tourist attractions, he might never know this atrocity was happening. *When I get out of here, everyone will know,* thought Amanda. *I'll tell them!*

"This is outrageous!" Amanda said to Martha, almost choking on her anger. She ripped the yellow triangle from her coat and threw it to the ground.

Martha squeezed her hand. "They want to humiliate us. They can do their worst, but they can't crush our hearts."

"You're right. We have to keep our faith in God."

Children, sensing their parents' fear, were crying. "Faith?" Martha cried. "You need to rethink this 'faith.' Look around you."

"Martha!" Dark blond brows drew together over Amanda's eyes. "What are you saying? Remember back when Miss Whitney took us to church, and we gave our hearts to Jesus?"

Martha drew in a breath of cold air and looked up into the leaden skies.

Walking sideways, Amanda stared into Martha's face. Her light blue eyes wavered. Amanda repeated fiercely, her voice barely above a whisper, "Remember?"

Martha's face showed her pain. "I remember," she said,

and looked away. "It was so long ago. I've tried to stay close to Christ since then. But where is He now?"

"He's here. He said He'd be."

A man in his thirties moved up in the crowd and put a hand on Uncle Jacob's shoulder. "Where are they taking us?" he asked, his dark eyes darting from face to face, averting his eyes from the guards hustling them through the gate.

Uncle Jacob turned a serious face to the man. "Why do you ask me? I don't know." The man shook his head, seeking answers in the faces around him, finding none.

As the Jewish group was herded through the streets of their own town, their silent fear turned to restless murmurs. Their former neighbors hung back in doorways, the younger ones watching curiously, some insolently from the sidewalks.

Amanda glanced at Tamara; she was just starting her family, but what was her future? She hadn't had time to retrieve a thing from her home. Amanda's first article would focus on this new family, and what these forced moves were doing to them.

The guards made the people hurry through town. They reached the outskirts of the small town in a few minutes. A black car slid up beside them, and an officer got out. He barked an order to the guards, who nudged the people forward. Those who balked were prodded and kicked. Terror and outrage, combined with the pushing, caused a crush of people in the narrow street.

Amanda shouldered through the crowd to approach the officer, when one of the guards pushed her back. Sick with their cruelty, she glared at him and said, "Where are you taking these people!"

With a brutal stare, he pushed her back again.

"I am an American citizen! I demand to know where you're taking us."

"Pah! You are no American. You are with this trash, so you march with the rest of them."

Refusing to turn away, she pointed to the officer. "I will speak with him!" She opened her purse and reached inside.

"Get back!" he roared. The officer glanced at the disturbance.

Amanda held her passport up, waving it. "I am an American citizen! I refuse to be treated like this." She fought to keep her voice calm and authoritative.

The officer approached. "What is going on here?"

Amanda shot the guard a cold look while he saluted. Before he could speak, she said, "Yes, what *is* going on here? I am an American citizen, and I find myself rounded up, shoved about like an animal." She looked behind her. "And what have these people done? Where are you taking them?"

The officer stared from under the black brim of his hat, then he took her passport. He calmly opened it, and flipped the pages, his lips thin with contempt. He gave her a measuring look, then put her passport in his pocket as if it were too filthy to look at.

Amanda took a deep breath to quell the panic welling in her throat.

"I will keep this and check your story. Now, get on the truck."

The guard grinned and gave her an extra hard shove. Amanda searched through the crowd. She spied Martha's blond head and went to her. "Where is Uncle Jacob, and the rest of the family?" she asked.

Martha's eyes were bleak as she pointed through the crowd, and then they heard a cry. Everyone turned to see a pillar of smoke rise from the other side of Eisenburg. "They're burning our homes!"

❧

Curley checked the instruments for the tenth time in as many minutes. The view outside hadn't changed. Low, flat clouds below, with glimpses of land between. All engine gauges were in the green. The airspeed indicator showed 120 mph, the engine sounded good; this sweet plane was performing beautifully.

But something was wrong. He knew it. He'd learned to trust his sixth sense when flying; it had saved his life more than once, especially on the stunt-flying circuit. Now, on his way to Holland, he felt more and more uncomfortable. Something was not right. Another check of the instrument panel and the steady drone of the engine confirmed that the problem was not in the plane. Then what?

Taking his mind off the plane's performance, he looked at the landmarks below. A bridge, a large stretch of water ahead. He'd just passed Hamburg. He stared out over the horizon. Amanda. He shook his head. She was on his mind too much. When this mission was over, he'd contact her and see where he stood. He didn't believe Delbert's statement that they were engaged.

He slipped the plane to the left to get a good view behind him and saw nothing but the sun rising. No German planes on his tail. His mission was safe, and he had an easy trip ahead. He reached behind his seat and took a candy bar from his flight bag. He peeled down the wrapper, telling himself there was no reason for this sense of uneasiness.

He bit off some chocolate and thought of Amanda again. He checked the map on his lap, putting a finger on his present location to note his progress. It didn't work. Amanda's face filled his mind. Coupled with the uneasiness he couldn't shake, he began to wonder if he should turn back.

If what he heard was true, and there was to be an uprooting of the Jews behind the wall, where would she be? Not anywhere near; not if she was smart and heeded his warning. No, she was all right. He smiled, thinking that at this minute she probably had her family with her at Frau Reinholdt's, eating strudel.

He finished his candy, and flew on toward Holland. *Go back.* He turned his head sharply. He'd heard the words as surely as if someone were sitting beside him. Even the engine throbbed: *Go back. Go back. Go back.* He frowned, as a vision of Amanda's face floated across his mind again.

Pressing the left rudder pedal and turning the control wheel, he made a 180-degree turn, retracing his progress. The closer he came, the more the urgency pulled at him. *Remember, God; I asked You to take care of her.*

After passing over the gray haze from Berlin's factories, he squinted at a column of smoke ahead. He hoped it was merely some farmer burning the chaff from his fields, but the smoke was billowing too high to be a burning field.

When he flew through the thin clouds low over Eisenburg, his suspicion was confirmed. The ghetto was on fire.

Curley knew he had to be careful; his mission, his very life could be in jeopardy, but he would have taxied down the main street, if it were wide enough, and rescued Amanda if she needed it. He knew now the strong urge to return was because somehow she was in trouble. And he grudgingly noted, the only trouble was in the ghetto where Amanda's family resided. He knew her—nosey reporter, stubborn champion of her family. She'd be right in the thick of things, trying to help.

He brought the plane down as close to town as he dared, making sure it was well hidden in the trees. He ran, parallel to the road about fifteen feet away, to avoid being seen.

Entering town from a side street, he pulled up his collar against the damp air, concealing his face, and made his way to Frau Reinhardt's. *Lord, let them be there in the parlor, away from the trouble. It will be so easy,* he thought, *to get Amanda—and her family, too, if they want—back to the plane and out of the country.*

He arrived at 11:15 A.M. Winnie, the elderly, red-haired woman, looked up as he stood at the parlor doorway. Her hand held a pen, poised over a journal. Smiling brightly, she said, "Hello there! We missed you at breakfast!"

"Thank you!" She was alone in the parlor. Curley pushed back his disappointment and smiled at her. Behind him he heard low voices and the rattle of dishes as the kitchen help set out the noon meal.

He was about to ask, when Winnie volunteered that Amanda hadn't been at breakfast either. "Her friend said the two of you most likely went out to see the sun rise." She craned her head to peer behind him. "She's not with you? Ah, well, perhaps she's still in her room." She touched her chin with the top of the pen thoughtfully and said, "I hope she's feeling well."

"Thank you," said Curley and nodded to her. "Good day."

He hurried up the stairs and knocked on Amanda's door.

A maid came from a room across the hall. "Miss Chase isn't in." She clutched a bundle of rolled-up sheets in her arms.

Curley looked briefly over his shoulder at her. *"Danke."* He went down the stairs, two at a time, the hair at his nape prickling. *Where is she? How will I find her?* He stood at the front door, rubbing his chin, when Delbert entered.

"Hello, old man!" he said, with a bright smile. "So, you're back. Did you and Amanda do some early sightseeing?" He pulled at the white muffler around his neck, unwinding it. "It's chilly out there."

"I saw smoke. What was burning?" asked Curley, ignoring Delbert's question.

Pulling off his gloves, Delbert answered. "Oh that. I heard that some apartments were burning. They wouldn't let anyone near; said it wasn't safe. The police escorted the poor folks who lived there through town, probably to a shelter."

"Which direction did they go?" asked Curley.

Delbert slapped the gloves across one hand and peered into the parlor. "What? Oh, south. Down that street by the park, the one with the shop that sells baroque figurines and paintings. Where's my dear fiancée, Amanda?"

Fiancée! He wouldn't believe Delbert's arrogant boasts. "Don't know. Excuse me." He reached past Delbert and pulled the door open. Looking both ways, he hurried away. He skirted the park, away from a policeman who stood with feet apart and hands clasped behind his back, watching the area.

He followed the street for a few blocks and, nearing the edge of town, saw nothing in the distance. If they had walked this street, it would have been over an hour ago at least. Keeping a low profile and walking quickly, but not so fast as to catch attention, he left town. As soon as he was back in the meadows, he ran to the plane.

Back in the air, he followed the winding road south of town. After a few minutes he saw them—a knot of about thirty people walking, with a black car behind them. He tipped the left wing and squinted at the group, but he wasn't close enough to pick out Amanda if she was in the crowd.

He followed the road, not daring to fly too low. The road curved its way south between low hills. He saw a bulky warehouse beside a railroad track. Three trucks and a black car were parked between the warehouse and a smaller building.

Curley flew on, scouring the area for a safe place to land and investigate. Orchards filled the hillsides, making it difficult to find a clear landing place, but the houses were few and far between, which made concealment easier.

Finally, he found a dirt road between rows of trees. Throttling back, he set the plane down, hoping the road was long enough for a takeoff later.

He tightened the wobbly tail wheel and was putting his wrench in the tool sack, when he heard the crunch of footsteps. He froze for an instant, then stood slowly and turned to face whoever was approaching.

fourteen

Grimly, Amanda marched with the Jews, passing hills with orchards rising on both sides of the road. The guards ordered them to walk in silence. Martha's remarks echoed in her mind. Why *had* God allowed their home to be taken, and now this?

A plane flew overhead, and she thought of Curley. *If only I'd believed all of what he said, and got my family away. I saw the evidence in the library; but I couldn't believe the Germans would brazenly evict the ghetto residents in broad daylight.*

Where was Curley? Probably in England by now, she figured, and wondered if she'd ever see him again. The memory of how he'd held her and kissed her last night warmly rippled through her. She glanced at Martha, attempting to divert her thoughts of Curley.

Amanda shivered in the weak sunlight as a chill wind stirred. She jammed her fists into her coat pocket, longing to get her notebook and pencil from her purse and take notes as she walked. Headlines flashed in her mind. *The Reich's Evil Side,* or *Hitler: Leader or Despot?* How she'd expose the cruelties going on here! First, she'd have to get out; and how would she do that? The ruthless officer had her passport in his pocket.

She remembered a Sunday school teacher saying God always provided a way out of trouble. *God, we need Your help now!*

Amanda and Martha were at the rear of the plodding group. Near the front, a young child suddenly stumbled. His mother, who held a toddler in her arms, stopped and encouraged him to stand. He whimpered as the guards told them to keep moving. Amanda scooped up the boy in her arms to avoid falling behind and incurring the guard's wrath. "Don't lose hope," she told the mother. "God will help us."

"Where are they taking us?" wailed the little boy.

"I don't know." Amanda hugged him close to her. "But as long as we have each other, we'll be all right."

When Amanda's steps slowed from the extra weight of the child, Martha carried him. They grew tired and thirsty, moving more laboriously as the day progressed into afternoon.

❧

Curley tensed as the man approached him. He was tall, well over six feet, thin as a prop blade, wearing a black short coat and faded black beret. The blue eyes that peered out from his wrinkled face were keen and observant.

His gaze flicked to the plane, scanning it from prop to tail wheel. "*Schones Flugzeug*," he breathed, then narrowed his gaze back to Curley. "*Aber was machen Sie hier?*" His clear eyes held no hint of malice or suspicion, merely a bright curiosity.

What should Curley tell him? He wouldn't lie, but he didn't need to spill the details of his mission. "My girlfriend is with a group of people walking the road over there." He gestured down the hill, "And I'm here to pick her up."

The man's eyes narrowed as he studied a thin straggle of grass which he nudged with his toe. After a moment he said, "You're American, aren't you?"

"Yes, I am." Curley bent to pick up his tool sack. Putting the wrench into it, he said, "I won't be here long, sir, and I'll pay you something for the bother."

The man looked up with a troubled expression. "No. No need to pay. This is bad business," he said, shaking his head.

Curley wondered what he meant, until he added, "Good and true citizens separated out, and for what? Where will it end?" He looked Curley square in the eye and said, "I will do all I can to help you." He shaded his eyes, looked down the row of trees, and whistled twice. "My grandson will help us."

Then he motioned Curley toward the plane. "Let's pull her back to a more secluded space, good for a quick takeoff."

A young man loped toward them, his eyes widening with surprised admiration when he saw the plane. The older man held out his hand to Curley. "My name is Horst Friedrich, and this is my grandson, Rutger."

Curley took his hand. "James Cameron. Thanks for the help," he said, shaking the young man's hand also.

Together they pulled the plane into a small grove, kicking aside some underbrush to make a clear path out. Walking down the hill together, Horst Friedrich told Curley he'd enlisted in 1914 as a pilot in the kaiser's war. He talked of the plane he flew, and they talked of Curley's Vega.

When they arrived at the farmhouse, Herr Friedrich offered Curley his truck. "It's a relic, like me, but reliable," he said. He waved aside Curley's protests. "Don't worry, I know you'll be back—your plane is here."

Rutger begged to go along, but his grandfather said no. Curley suspected the man wasn't sure Curley could successfully rescue his girlfriend and return the truck.

He quickly caught up with the group struggling to keep ahead of the two black cars behind them. He pushed the pad in the middle of the round steering wheel, and a baritone bark came from the truck's horn. The black cars ignored it.

Curley pulled the truck off the road and got out. He ran to one of the cars and tapped on its window, walking to keep up. The guard pretended not to see him, then finally rolled the window down a few inches and ordered him to get away.

"Stop! I need to talk with you. *Bitte*." His German was minimal, and he hoped adding the word "please" would help.

The guard rolled the window up and stared straight ahead. The car continued moving, with Curley persistently tapping on the window again and again.

Finally the guard ordered the driver to stop, and opened the door, almost knocking Curley over. "What is this? You are interrupting state business. Get out of here." The guard rested his hand on his holster to reinforce his demand.

The group huddled in the cold, their shoulders heaving with exhaustion. "One of your. . .group does not belong here. My friend, Amanda Chase. She is a visiting American citizen."

The guard's eyes narrowed. "What lies are these you tell? These criminals are none of your business."

Curley bit back his anger to keep from asking the man what crime the small children had done. Another officer, from the other car, approached and asked what caused the delay.

They commanded Curley to go, but he refused to leave unless Amanda was with him. He took a chance that they were not ready to risk exposing their present activity. They threatened to arrest him. He told them he had friends waiting for him to bring Amanda back.

Amanda approached them, and Curley smiled, calling her to join them. The other guards kept the people in the middle of the road, moving them to one side when a car passed.

"Hello, Amanda," said Curley with a smile. "What are you doing here?"

"That's what I'd like to know!" She put her hands on her hips and glared at the guard who had her passport. "I told you," she said to him, "I'm an American citizen and I want to go home."

The guard arched an eyebrow, and patted his pocket. "We'll check your passport." He folded his arms across his chest, "and if you really are an American citizen, then you may go."

"Listen." Curley curbed his temper. "I sympathize with your efforts to relocate so many families devastated by fire, but I'm a businessman, and don't have time for passport checking and other tedious delays." He clenched his fists. "Let the girl go."

Amanda stepped closer to Curley and touched his arm. "Thanks for coming back." To the guard she said, "Please believe me, I'm not one of these people. If you keep me you could get into great trouble with your superiors. My father is an influential man who knows President Roosevelt, and he would not rest until I was released."

"Lies!" screamed the guard. "Get back in the group."

"I will not." Amanda brought her face close to his. "Shoot me now, because I won't walk in your stupid parade anymore."

She kept her voice low to keep it from wavering. She longed to demand her passport back, but feared pressing this guard too far.

After an awkward moment, the guard jerked his head toward the car, ordering the others back inside and the driver to move along. "Move, you vermin scum!" he yelled to the people huddled in the cold road.

Martha, holding the child in her arms, approached. "Amanda, what's happening?"

The guard shoved her, and she fell, clutching the child so he wouldn't be hurt. Amanda started forward, but Curley pulled her back. "Come on. You can't help her now."

He was right. She couldn't help Martha by being arrested, but as a free person she might help. She walked away, but shouted back to Martha, "I won't leave you here!"

With tears distorting her vision she pulled at her coat buttons. By the time they got to the old truck she had her coat and jacket open, and the lenses out of her pockets.

Curley opened the door for her. "What are you doing?"

"Documenting," she muttered. By the time he climbed in behind the steering wheel, she was fastening the lens on her camera. "Drive as close as you can," she said.

"They have guns, remember," Curley warned. "If I see one drawn, we're making a hasty exit." He turned the truck in a wide circle, almost miring it in the soft dirt on the side of the road as he jockeyed them into position for perfect photos. "Be quick. We can't make another pass."

Amanda wiped her eyes and blinked back the tears, then snapped the heartrending scene. As they sped away she leaned out of the truck for one more shot.

When they were too far away for more pictures, she drew her head in out of the biting wind, set the camera on the seat, and rolled up the window. "Brrr. Does this truck have a heater?" With cold fingers she buttoned her jacket, then her coat.

Curley reached beneath his seat, and drew out a pair of stiff gardening gloves. "I kicked these under the seat when I got in. They'll soften up once you get them on."

Amanda pulled on the cold gloves, then wrapped her coat closer around her ankles. Looking at the confident set of Curley's shoulders, the strong lines of his profile, she felt his strength as he drove them away from danger. "How. . .where did you get this truck? I thought you left this morning. How did you know where to find me?"

He used the grin that was always there on the edge of his mouth, as he said, "Hey, one at a time!" His movements were swift and graceful as he shifted the gears and steered the truck expertly down the country road.

She relaxed back against the seat, relief flooding her to be in his presence. "Right. A good reporter asks one question at a time." The gloves were beginning to warm her hands.

"I did leave this morning," he said, leaning slightly to look out the rearview mirror. "But something made me return—don't ask me what. If I had to guess, I'd say it was the Holy Spirit. All I know for certain is I just knew I had to come back. The truck belongs to a local farmer, and we're returning it as soon as I make a quick trip into town."

Amanda twisted in the seat, looking back, worry etching her brow. Doubt ate at her; had she been right to leave her family behind? Maybe she could have somehow brought them with her. Or maybe she should have stayed with them, no matter what the cost. Tears blurred her eyes. "Stop the truck!" she cried suddenly, reaching for the door handle. "I won't leave my family to those butchers!"

"Hey! Calm yourself," said Curley. The road had turned, and the group behind them was no longer visible. He pulled the truck over to the side of the road, keeping the motor idling.

Bracing his left elbow on the steering wheel, he reached over and took her hand from the handle. "Think. Alone you can't stop them. You could get yourself hurt, or share whatever fate the Nazis have in store for their captives."

"But. . ." She looked back in anguish.

Curley squeezed her hand. "I know. We can't leave them

there." He reached up and cupped her chin, turning her face to his. "I have a plan, which I hope will free them all from whatever those thugs have planned."

"How? What can we do?"

His fingers lingered against the softness of her cheek. The shine in her eyes which a moment ago threatened to overflow into tears now regained the intellectual curiosity he'd first noticed about her. A memory flashed through his mind from many years ago, of a much younger girl with the same curiosity mixed with intelligence, looking up at him with admiration.

He slid his hand down, pulling her collar closer around her neck. "First I have to make a quick trip into town to discover for sure where they are taking them." He turned back toward the steering wheel, put the truck in gear, and started forward.

Amanda leaned toward him, peering into his face. "Who would tell you *that?*"

The truck swayed as he steered it back onto the roadway. "Trust me," he said. "We don't have much time, so I'll drop you off at Frau Reinhardt's. Gather up your things while I find out what we need to know. Then we'll make a mad dash back here to put my plan into action."

"What plan? Tell me!"

He rubbed his thumb on the steering wheel, thinking, and finally decided to tell her. "First," he said, "if I'm right, we have to wait until it's dark and very late."

He sketched the highlights of a plan and in response to her concerns, promised to tell it in detail, later.

Soon the old truck chugged up to Frau Reinhardt's rooming house. Amanda slipped off the gardening gloves and laid them on the seat. "See you in five minutes," she said.

Curley was already turning the corner as she entered the foyer. She ran up the stairs and down the hall to her room, thankful for Curley's intervention into this sordid situation.

Quickly entering the room she breathed a quick prayer. *God, help us. We're against evil forces here that I don't understand. Without Your help we could ruin everything.* She threw one of her suitcases on the bed and snapped it open.

She yanked her warmest clothes off their hangers and stuffed them in, along with her cosmetics which were hastily thrown into their satin-lined drawstring bag. The suitcase refused to latch. She pulled her tweed jacket from the jumble of clothes. *Someone will get a lot of use from this,* she thought, laying it across the pillows.

She forced the suitcase shut and slung her purse strap over her shoulder. Reaching into the closet, she grabbed the camera case, then picked up the suitcase. At the door she took one last look before leaving. The room was it was as when she arrived, except for the jacket lying on the pillows and the clothes that still hung in the closet.

Downstairs, she was almost out the door when Delbert rose from a chair in the parlor and eyed her suitcase. With a wave of his elegant fingers he gestured toward it. A shocked petulance crept into his voice as he asked, "Honey—oh, sorry. Amanda, my dear. What does this mean? Are you leaving?"

Amanda set the suitcase down, seeing him clearly for the first time. After all their years as friends she felt she never really knew him. Yet, somehow he believed she would someday become his wife. He stood before her, his pretty-boy face lit from within with selfish ambition.

"Amanda?" He cleared his throat, and she realized she was still staring at him.

"I've found my family," she said, "and I'm going to them." She reached into her purse and drew out some money. "I'm paid up with Frau Reinhardt, but would you be a pal and give her this? And could you take care of the rest of my stuff that's up in my room? Have it shipped home for me?"

"Of course I will." He brought his hand back to his chest. "But I'll take care of your bill."

She pressed the money into his sweater pocket. "Really, Delbert, I insist." She pulled the door open, and he grabbed her suitcase before she could and went out with her.

"Where can I reach you?" He took her arm and turned her to face him. "After all, Amanda, I came here to be with you, to assist you however I could." When she pulled away from him, he added, "Remember, your father entrusted me with your care."

Amanda wished the old truck would appear. "So you said, and I said I was grateful for your concern. If you'll remember, I also told you I don't need a baby-sitter."

"Now see here—"

"No. *You* see here. I don't need you, Delbert. Go back to Boston." At his look of shock at her uncharacteristic outburst, she softened somewhat and added, "Please!"

As if on cue, the truck chugged around the corner and slid to a stop in front of them. Amanda opened the door before Delbert could do it for her. She slung the suitcase on the floor, put the camera case on the seat and climbed in. Curley leaned around her and nodded to Delbert.

Pulling the door shut, she looked straight ahead and said, "Let's go!" Curley gave her a curious look, stepped on the clutch, put the truck in gear, and they sped away.

fifteen

Curley skillfully sped down the narrow streets, braking suddenly in front of the bakery shop. "Stay here. I'll be right back." Shifting into neutral, he flung open the door and jumped out, leaving the motor running. Amanda's stomach rumbled, reminding her she hadn't eaten anything since the cup of tea and cookie at Aunt Esther's that morning. So much had happened, that the morning's events seemed ages ago.

In less than a minute, Curley came out with two full gunnysacks. He slung them into the back of the truck and went back for more. Finished, he jumped back into the truck and scanned the street ahead, then checked the rearview mirror, put the truck in gear, then pulled away. Soon Eisenburg faded into the twilight behind them.

"What's in the bags?" asked Amanda.

Solemnly watching the road ahead, Curley answered, "Apples, bread, rolls, jelly, whatever the baker could assemble in a hurry."

Amanda pressed her stomach to keep it from feeling too empty, and nodded. "Good idea. The soldiers certainly won't feed those poor people." She busied herself by putting the camera and pieces back into its case.

Curley's jaw muscle flexed as he clenched his teeth. "No doubt about it," he said.

Surprised by the stern tone of his voice, Amanda glanced at him. He wasn't just a pretty flyboy. Suddenly his boyishly handsome profile showed an inherent strength and power she hadn't noticed before. He gripped the steering wheel tighter and stepped hard on the gas pedal, urging the truck to move faster.

"How are you going to get this food to the people?"

He glanced at her. "Part of the plan."

She felt the shock of power blazing from his hazel eyes, and she knew that nothing would stop him from taking food to the Jews.

He switched the lights on, and in a few minutes he turned off the road, into a long dirt driveway. He stopped behind a white peak-roofed house.

A tall older gentleman and a younger similar-looking man stepped out of the porch shadows and approached the truck. The older gentleman leaned down and looked past Curley to Amanda. "I see you got her, *mein Herr.*"

The young man's eyes widened as he caught sight of Amanda. "Oohh," he breathed, then hastily rubbed his chin and turned nonchalantly as if seeing a beautiful woman was nothing new.

Curley turned off the motor and lights, plunging them into almost total darkness. He got out of the truck, and Amanda reached for her door handle, but the young man suddenly appeared and opened it for her.

She pulled her coat collar up against the biting cold as Curley introduced the older gentleman as Horst and the younger as Rutger Friedrich. They shook hands and exchanged smiles before walking into the lamp-lit kitchen. Coal embers glowed brightly in an iron stove against one wall, warming the room somewhat. Washed dishes were neatly stacked beside the sink, and a dark wood table sat against the outside wall.

"Rutger and I are alone for a few days while my wife is away at her sister's." Herr Friedrich pulled two more cups from the cupboard. "So, you will be taking off soon?" Rutger brought them each a cup of hot tea. Amanda brought in some dark bread from the truck.

Curley took a sip of the hot brew and shook his head. "No. Not while those people are captives."

Amanda curled her hands around the cup, warming them for a moment, darting him a grateful look. "How are we going to free them?"

"It's going to be dangerous. You must wait in the plane

while I go."

"You don't know my uncle and aunt. I have to go with you."

Curley shook his head. "I saw you with your cousin, so that's not a problem." He leaned toward Herr Friedrich, relying on Amanda for German phrases, and laid out his plan.

After intense discussion, they determined that Rutger would go along to distract the guards while Curley did his part. Herr Friedrich nodded his assent and said, "We do nothing but we ask God to go with us. You have no objection to that?"

Curley smiled. "Not at all. He's with me everywhere I go."

"How about you, miss?" Herr Friedrich asked Amanda, looking at her keenly.

"No. It's fine." She glanced at Curley, impressed by his faith. *That must be why he has such a calm attitude about all this,* she thought, remembering with chagrin that she didn't always remember to trust in God, knowing the serene feeling that He had everything in control.

After a prayer that lifted her courage, they hugged each other. Rutger smiled and said, "God's been saving His people for generations. This isn't exactly the Red Sea, but He'll do something great tonight. Wait and see!"

They all laughed, then solemnly prepared for the night ahead.

Outside, a cold, silvery full moon hung over the bare branches of trees, silhouetted on the hillside. Horst and Rutger went to work on the truck while Amanda followed Curley along a path up the hill behind the house. He carried her suitcase and a flashlight to illuminate the path ahead, while she shouldered her purse and camera case, carefully stepping over the uneven ground.

As soon as they reached the top of the hill, she grabbed Curley's arm and he turned to face her. She steadied her camera case to stop it from swinging and glared at him. "You can't leave me behind. I need to go with you."

He set the suitcase down, taking her hand in his. He smiled. This was his feisty Amanda, ready to jump into the fray. He'd been worried by her earlier silence in the kitchen. "You can't. They'd recognize you in an instant."

"I'll stay in the shadows. They won't even see me."

"We can't risk it. You stay in the plane, I go to the rescue."

She stared at him, unable to look away. She'd never met a man like this. So gentle and loving at times, yet so hard-headed as he was now. She admired his boldness and had no doubts that he'd do exactly as he planned. But her mind was made up. "You'll have to tie me down to make me stay here."

Curley dragged his gaze away from hers to keep from faltering. "If you want to fly out of here with me, you'll go with my plan." He dropped her hand and continued walking.

She stood in the silent darkness, stunned for an instant. Then she ran after him. "Listen, mister, I'm not some dainty little woman who'll faint at the first sign of trouble."

He looked back at her, arching one brow. "No?" He shook his head, leading her through shoulder-high bushes to the plane. He opened the cargo door, placing her suitcase inside, then opened the passenger door.

Amanda slung her camera case and purse up behind the co-pilot seat and turned to Curley with a sigh. "Listen, I didn't mean to sound flippant. But I. . .I need to go. This is my family!" She liked his decisiveness, but there must be some way to convince him of her need to be involved.

Curley made the mistake of gazing down at her, watching the play of emotions on her face. He suppressed a sigh. She had, after all, gone right into the ghetto in search of her family. He imagined her stalking dark Boston streets, searching for a story, and knew she was right. She needed to go.

He turned away from her and ran a hand through his hair, not sure if her foray into the ghetto had been bravery or foolishness. "You heard the plan. The guards have guns. People could get hurt if something goes wrong."

She looked up at him. "I know," she said softly. "But remember, we prayed, and God will protect us."

Curley lightly touched his fingertips to her chin and then leaned down, swiftly kissing her mouth. Then he turned abruptly and went to the other side of the plane where he opened the door and retrieved a flare, a can of gasoline, and a few small tools. He pulled the plane forward a few feet so it faced a makeshift runway for a quick, clear takeoff.

≈

With Rutger driving, soon they were turning onto the roadway and heading south on the road she'd walked earlier. After about five miles, Rutger turned off the lights. He slowed enough to peer carefully at the moonlit stretch of road.

"It's there, on our left," he whispered, pointing. Curley and Amanda bent their heads to their knees, so Rutger would seem to be driving alone.

Curley slowly opened the door a fraction of an inch. "Remember, if I don't get back right away, go on without me. I'll make my way back somehow. But don't wait!" Rutger nodded, driving past the turnoff. He turned the truck around and came back, pulling off the road.

Rutger hopped out and reached into the truck bed, grabbing one of the sacks. Shouldering it, he walked down the gravel road toward two small buildings. Lights glowed from within one of them. The other stood dark. He grinned. The German guards would love the treats he was bringing.

Once Rutger had disappeared into the shadows, Amanda and Curley quietly pushed the open door and slipped out of the truck. Curley grabbed his flare and gasoline and a sack of bakery goods from the truck bed. Amanda took another sack, and they tiptoed toward the large warehouse straight ahead and down an incline.

They stayed close to the bushes, away from gravel that would crunch loudly with each step. They reached the warehouse and moved stealthily along the wall nearest the road, looking for windows or some kind of opening. They found steps leading down to a metal door. Curley descended to investigate. The door was rusty, looking as if it hadn't been used in years. Amanda stood straining her ears, listening for sounds of movement. It was eerily quiet. Curley ascended the stairs and they continued to the corner of the building and scrutinized the next wall. A small vent lay open a few inches off the ground.

On the other side of the building, facing the railroad tracks, they found a loading dock. The faint light from a smaller building illuminated the area.

Curley ducked back. "This is a good place to leave the sacks," he whispered to Amanda. "Stay put while I check out the other side of this building."

Amanda nodded, but after a few moments she crawled back to the spot where they'd seen the vent. She bent down, finally lying on the ground to get closer. She heard a sniffling noise and a groan. She'd found them! She picked up a pebble and tapped lightly on the wire screen. She waited, but she didn't receive an answer. Pulling her pencil out of her pocket, she stuck it inside, making contact with something.

She poked again, hoping it wasn't merely a sack of grain. The object moved. *Please don't be a rat or a cat.* She pushed her pencil in again, startled when it was drawn out of her hand.

"Hello!" she whispered as loudly as she dared. "Is someone there?"

Something or someone shifted on the other side of the wall.

"Hello. Is someone there?" A frightened child's voice came from the square hole.

Amanda breathed a sigh of relief. *Thank God.* "Shhh. Get your father or mother quickly." She heard scuffling, and then another voice came through the wires. "Who's there?"

Amanda told the person who she was, and asked him to get Uncle Jacob. Soon he was there, head to the floor, talking to her. She told him of the escape plan, the bread beside the loading door, and asked him to keep the people calm and quiet.

🙘

Curley hid in the shadows, hugging the wall on the other side of the building. He found a boarded window with an open slot large enough to talk through. His message was the same as Amanda's to her uncle. When he finished, he crept silently back to where he'd left Amanda. There was a moment of pure panic when he couldn't find her. He finally spotted her; she lay unmoving in the shadows. He advanced slowly toward her, relieved to hear her faint whispers and an answering voice.

He motioned to her to be ready to run back to the truck and he slowly made his way to the loading dock wall. There, he unlatched the loading door's bolt and slid it from its rings. Then he crawled across the loading dock and pried the bolt loose, sliding it from its rings slowly so as to minimize the noise. He glanced up at the light over the door of the guards' building, wishing he had some way to put it out. The weak light was just enough to be dangerous.

He froze as a guard opened the door and walked out of the small building. The guard turned to speak to someone inside, and Curley slipped around the corner into the shadows. A second guard came out, followed by another and Rutger.

"*Ja,* you tell the baker we liked his gift," one of the guards said as he adjusted his holster strap, preparing to make his rounds.

"I will." Rutger held the empty gunny sack in his hand, walking after them. "I could come tomorrow and bring more."

They shook their heads. "We will not be here tomorrow. You go now."

Rutger slowly walked up the road. He looked about casually, not wanting to appear nosey, but obviously wondering where Amanda and Curley were.

Curley waited until the guards walked behind the building. He closed his eyes, praying that Amanda had gotten out of the way. Then he moved around the supply shed, dripping gas down the walls, and along its base. When he finished he moved behind the warehouse and lit the flare.

A guard rounded the building. "Halt!" he shouted, and started running toward Curley, who tossed the flare and dived to the ground. With a whoosh and flash of heat the supply shed was instantly engulfed in flames. Guards shouted. More came running out of the office building. They pointed their guns into the darkness, momentarily confused. Then a voice rose above the others, giving orders.

On his belly, Curley used his elbows to ease himself forward. He worked his way along the ground beside the building, rolling into the underground doorway. Jumping to his feet he pushed the door with all his strength. It groaned and scraped loudly, but the sounds were lost in the roar of the fire and the shouts of the scattering guards.

৵

When Amanda heard the guards talking to Rutger, she'd slid the two gunny sacks of breadstuff toward the door which someone inside had pushed up a few inches. The bags were slowly pulled inside. She crawled through the bushes and made her way along the road to the truck. She spotted Rutger, but didn't dare call out to him. He reached the vehicle first, spying her at the same time the supply shed went up in flames. Amanda dashed the last few feet to the truck, praying for Curley's safety. The Germans sprinted about, shouting orders, moving cars, and throwing pails of water on the fire.

Amanda and Rutger could do nothing more but wait for Curley. Minutes passed. Rutger paced impatiently. Finally he turned to her, frowning. "They know I'm here, so I'll go tell them I want to help," he said. "I'll find out what happened to Curley."

"No! Don't! What if they think you're the one who set the fire?" Her plea fell into the darkness. She was alone.

The blazing building lit up the area, and Amanda knew she had to keep down, but it was agony not to look. She caught her breath, heaving a mental sigh of relief when first one, then another car drove by the truck and sped down the road. "Come on! Come on!" she whispered, clenching her fists. "God, help them!"

She heard a light tapping and, lying across the seat, she opened the driver's door. A familiar face greeted her. "Uncle Jacob!"

Her uncle huddled beside the truck, his arm leaning on the running board. His eyes were wild and frightened. Amanda stretched the door open a few more inches. "Are you all here?" she asked.

He nodded. "In the bushes."

"Good." She glanced nervously up the road. "As soon as Curley and Rutger get here, climb in the back."

He nodded, "But we must hurry!" Then he slipped away, back into the bushes.

Less than two minutes later Rutger climbed into the truck, frowning.

"Where's Curley?"

"I couldn't find him! I'm sorry, Amanda. He has disappeared."

Amanda peeked out the window. Seeing no one, she looked frantically up and down the road. "They'll be back any minute, with help."

"I know," Rutger agreed. "We have to go."

"We can't leave him!" cried Amanda.

"It's what he told us to do," Rutger insisted.

"But—"

"I don't want to leave him either, but if anyone can get himself out of this jam and back to his plane, Curley can."

Turning the trees into black skeletons, the flames leaped into the sky with a sickly orange vengeance. Amanda looked back at the bushes and saw her aunt peering out at her. "You're right. We have to trust Curley to make it." She motioned to Aunt Esther, and in a few seconds they'd all scrambled from the bushes onto the back of the truck.

Rutger started the truck, hesitated a moment, looking at the burning buildings. Now the warehouse was in flames. He didn't see Curley. He put the truck in gear. It lurched forward, and soon they were on their way back to the farmhouse.

Amanda looked back, hoping to see Curley, but there was nothing but the surging flames. She saw two people dash across the road, and she wished them well. In the truck bed all that remained visible were blankets and burlap bags covering lumps of supposed farm products.

&

When Curley closed the metal door darkness engulfed him. He pointed his flashlight at the wall and pushed its button. Nothing happened. He tried again. Nothing. His fingers explored the metal cylinder and found the glass and bulb broken. The darkness grew oppressive and ominous with its silence. He struck a match, looking around, quickly assessing his surroundings. He was in a small vaultlike room, about ten feet square. Two shelves along one wall held several boxes of musty papers and a few cans that were so rusted he couldn't make out their labels.

He checked his watch. Eleven-twenty. The match died out. He stood in the darkness, waiting, knowing he couldn't go out yet. He heard muffled footsteps above, sounds of prisoners escaping. Hours seemed to pass before all he could hear was his own breathing, and the slight movement of his foot on the dusty floor.

A cold, clammy feeling crept up from his belly to encompass him. He felt powerless to stop it. He stared straight ahead, straining to see something, anything, but there was nothing. Only a loathsome opacity. Fragments from old nightmares floated into his mind. The pain that started when his mother died. He was four years old. He didn't remember much about her, but the aching sadness. He and his father had been close.

Then his father's death in the mine shaft, a freak accident of boulders and crushing debris. Curley's terrible dreams about it were coming true.

He had learned to hide his grief with nonchalance and an exaggerated sense of independence. Deciding never to need anyone, since no one would be there anyway, he'd gotten by, living where he could, finally ending up in Johnny Westmore's hangar. Johnny had taken him under his wing, literally, taught him to fly and to trust God to be with him always. Johnny had became the closest thing to family Curley had.

He shook himself and pulled out another match. *I'm not alone,* he thought, *I'll get through this just like I always have. By my wits and with God's help.* He forced himself to put the match back without lighting it and face the darkness. He didn't need a crutch, not even the match. This might be the worst predicament of his life, but he'd manage.

He felt the darkness closing around him, suffocating like a vise of black death. He squeezed his eyes shut, imagining the free feeling of soaring over the clouds in an open cockpit. He was an eagle, far above problems on the ground, strong, needing no one. The image faded, pushed out by the oppressive blackness, leaving him gasping and groping for the door.

He clenched his fists, fighting off the feeling of being nine years old again. Of hearing the imaginary sounds of men screaming as a mine shaft fell in on them. Of fearing he heard his father's screams. "Oh God!" he breathed. The oppression loosened a little. Curley closed his eyes and said into the darkness, "Yea, though I walk through the valley of the shadow of death I will fear no evil." His shoulders relaxed.

Johnny used to tell him there was no shame in admitting a need for God's help. *I know I'm no lone eagle, needing no one. I know You're there, God. Thank You.*

He took a deep breath and stood for a moment, savoring the feeling of peace. Then he once more took out a match and struck it, checking the time. Eleven forty-two. Twenty-two minutes had elapsed since he'd shut himself in this musty vault. It seemed like twenty-two hours. The air was getting thicker and warmer by the minute. He wondered if Amanda, her family, and Rutger were all right. He hoped they hadn't waited for him.

He smiled. Amanda was no frail female. He couldn't think of any other girls who he'd even consider letting come with him into this situation; and she'd done it with such aplomb. A glow of determination in her eyes, courage in that thrust-forward little chin, strength to tread where angels feared, and beauty. *She's the real article,* he told himself. Suddenly he couldn't wait to get to her and get his arms around her.

The door handle felt warm. Carefully, he pulled the door open a fraction of an inch. A flame curled downward, blocking his escape. Pulling at his jacket sleeve, he wrapped it around his hand and pushed the rapidly heating metal door. The coast was clear, so he dashed out through the flames and up the steps.

He stepped right into the path of a German guard carrying an empty bucket in each hand.

sixteen

The guard stumbled as Curley ran into him. He dropped the buckets and slapped at Curley's shoulder. Raising a fist to strike back, Curley suddenly realized the fierce burning he felt on his shoulder was his smoldering jacket. Together he and the guard put it out.

An acrid gray smoke drifted up from the burning leather. Someone dashed past them with pails of sloshing water. Before the guard could question him, Curley gestured wildly down the steps he'd just come up, then picked up the discarded pails.

His eyes darted from side to side, assessing the area. The truck had gone with Amanda, Rutger, and, he hoped, her family. Though adrenaline and tension fueled his alertness, he was relieved that Amanda was out of harm's way. He worried about her getting into another dilemma. Their safe escape depended on his getting out of here soon.

He ran with the pails to the water tower. Orange flames crept up the building where the prisoners had been kept, sending sparks flying out the narrow upper windows.

A truck skidded down the road, off the highway, the people in the back jumping out before it stopped. Curley pushed the pails under the water spout, filling them. He was relieved that others were so intent on getting water to the fire there was no conversation.

He rushed to the track side of the warehouse and sloshed water up the wall. The door was open and there was no sign of the Jews. Thank God, they'd escaped. The guards, plus volunteers, were getting the fire under control. A middle-aged man ran past him, toward the building, smothering the fire with a sack full of sand. Curley handed him the pails and ran toward the guards' small hut.

There was no fire here. No guards either. They were directing volunteers and dousing bushes and the warehouse. Their motorcycles sat next to the building. The black car was gone.

From the dark bushes behind the hut, Curley scanned the scene. Twenty or more people ran to and from the water tower. Others beat the bushes with blankets and burlap bags to choke the fire. The supply shed smoldered from its burned, blackened stubble, a pocket of water seeping from its foundation.

He heard voices near and froze. The captain came toward the guard hut, gazing from the fiery pandemonium to the bushes behind him, where Curley crouched. *"Der Amerikaner ist hier.* Bring him to me!"

Curley couldn't hear every word, but he caught the meaning. The guard was told to bring the American to his captain. As soon as the soldiers left, he sneaked toward the motorcycles and chose one without a sidecar. He guided it quietly on a well-worn footpath around the back, behind the bushfire. The flickering flames gave enough light to get the motorcycle up to the road.

He stood on the crank three times, but the machine didn't catch. He was raising it a fourth time when an oncoming motorcycle's light shined on him. Behind him, a guard ran toward him, shouting and gesturing.

Suddenly the oncoming motorcycle turned sharply and pulled up beside him. Curley shoved the kickstand down and turned, ready to fight for his life, if necessary. But it was Rutger's cheerful face smiling at him.

Rutger slapped the fender behind him. "Get on!"

Guards down the hill were wheeling their motorcycles away from the guard hut. Curley hopped on the back and held onto Rutger's seat. "Step on it, boy!"

Rutger tore off down the road as fast as the cycle would go. Curley looked back and spotted headlights behind them. At first he thought it was a car, but the lights moved independently, and he knew there were two motorcycles following him. He and Rutger leaned into the wind, keeping the accelerator wide open.

About a hundred yards before Friedrich's driveway Rutger slowed, and turned off the road onto an overgrown lane. A minute later he turned off the lights, but he kept a steady pace as he twisted and wound along the dirt road.

The cloudy moonlight was barely enough for him to see to steer between the bushes. The guards' motorcycles thundered past the turnoff.

Rutger rounded a bend, flicked the lights on, and gunned the engine again. They bounced through the orchard and he cut the engine and coasted into the clearing where the plane sat.

They had only minutes before the guards doubled back, found the side road, and caught up with them. Curley vaulted off the motorcycle and grabbed the handlebars from Rutger. One of the motorcycles rumbling toward them sputtered and whined, sounding as if it had slid off the path into the dirt. The other one bore down on them.

Rutger glanced uneasily behind them toward the approaching roar. Curley took his arm and pushed him back into the shadows. "Go home. I don't want you involved in this. Get back!"

"Yes, sir." Rutger slipped silently into the shadows, saying over his shoulder, "Everyone is in the plane, waiting for you."

"Good job! Now you must go. *Go!*" The moon had gone behind a cloud and Curley stood, facing the oncoming guard, then straightened his shoulders and watched the light loom brighter. "Lord, help me," he muttered. "And keep Amanda in the plane."

❧

Amanda watched Curley face the motorcycle leaping into the clearing. In the surrounding darkness the scene looked as if it were a stage play unfolding before her. But this was no act.

"What's happening? What is it?" Aunt Esther's voice rose to an hysterical pitch.

"It's all right," said Amanda softly, failing to keep the fear from her voice. "Mr. Cameron is here to fly us out. Sit back, and. . ."

"But I—"

"Now, now, Mother. Come, lean against me," soothed Uncle Jacob. Aunt Esther allowed him to pull her into his arms, while Tamara, Nathan, and the baby huddled together in the rear of the plane. Martha's head touched Amanda's as they peered out the small window.

"What's he going to do?" asked Martha, reaching for Amanda's hand and clutching it tightly.

"Shh!" Amanda chose her words carefully to cover her own growing alarm. "He'll be all right. Just keep our passengers quiet. Please."

She could tell by the guard's slow, deliberate motions as he stood his motorcycle on its stand that he felt he was in total control. He left the light on, pointed his pistol at Curley, and motioned toward the plane. Amanda ducked down, even though she couldn't be seen. When she looked again, Curley had edged away from the plane. He and the guard faced off, looking as motionless as chess pieces.

She touched her forehead to the cool window and said a quick prayer for all of them.

"Explain yourself! *Wer sind Sie?* Who are you? Why is this plane here?" The guard motioned to the plane with his Luger.

"Etwas langsammer, bitte," said Curley after a long tension-filled minute. "I speak very little German." He assumed a relaxed pose, but every sense was on alert.

The guard backed up to his motorcycle, all the time keeping the gun on Curley. His stare lingered as he pulled a flashlight from the saddlebag and snapped the light on. "I will inspect the plane before I escort you back to my captain."

In a voice of authority, Curley said, "That plane is RAF property, and off limits."

"You are on German soil! You will do as I say." He shone his light from the propeller to the tail of the plane, stepping closer to it.

A sweat broke out on Curley's neck. Time was running out. The guard's momentary attention on the plane gave him an opening. He leaped at the man, but the guard turned, raising his gun. Curley grabbed the wrist holding the weapon.

Amanda could scarcely breathe as she watched Curley move with incredible lightning speed. He and the guard scuffled, the flashlight beam darting crazily about until Curley forced the guard to the ground. They rolled in the dirt, struggling for the gun. She watched in horror as the guard pinned Curley beneath him. The flashlight's beam shone uselessly into the trees.

Curley seemed to relax and give up for an instant, then he surged up, threw the guard off him, and knocked the gun from his hand. It skittered across the dirt under the plane's wing. The guard lunged and Curley slugged him. He staggered back, then lowered his head and charged Curley.

"I've got to help," said Amanda, reaching for the door handle.

"No!" Martha grabbed her sleeve.

Amanda gently pulled her hand away. "Keep calm! I'll be all right." She opened the door and slid into the cold darkness.

The gun glinted dully beneath the plane's wing. She picked it up. It felt like a piece of ice in her hand.

Holding it in both hands, she pointed it toward the guard. In German she said, "The only thing I know about guns is that if I pull this trigger, it shoots. So don't move, or you'll make me nervous, and you could get hurt." She breathed deeply, stilling the fear tensing her chest.

Curley moved to her side, his eyes on her face. "You surprise me, sweetheart."

The German snarled an obnoxious epithet, and Curley leveled a sudden, icy glare at him. "The lady means business. Keep quiet."

Anger faded from the guard's red face as he watched Amanda's hands shaking. She stood, arms outstretched, pointing the gun at him. To Curley she said, "I'll keep him here until the plane is ready to go. Hurry!" Curley picked up the flashlight and set it on the guard's motorcycle seat, so that it spotlighted him.

The guard's eyes flickered as he watched Curley leave the circle of light.

Amanda moved the gun slightly. "Don't try anything," she warned. She moved her eyes as far to the right as she could, following Curley, but he had ducked beneath the plane. She heard the door close, and fought down her fear.

The guard glared at her, tensing as if for a leap in her direction. Heavy, almost clumsy footsteps heading in their direction made him smile.

Amanda kept the gun pointed on him. The man's smile faded as Rutger walked into the light. "Who are you?" the man demanded, his voice rising to a shriek.

"I am a fellow countryman, looking for my motorcycle." Rutger looked from the guard to the plane. "Why is that here?"

"You idiot! This is not Der Fuhrer's plane!"

"Then what—"

"Both of you keep quiet," said Amanda.

Rutger peered toward Amanda. "Who's that?" A cloud drifted in front of the moon, casting unearthly shadows. The guard stood in eerie light, and Rutger, half in shadow, half in the light.

"Stop asking questions!" screeched the guard.

"You sound like the guard at the roadside. He is injured," said Rutger, glancing meaningfully toward Amanda.

She pulled in a deep, shaky breath, her arms beginning to ache. *Oh, please, Curley, start the plane!* She hadn't known there was a second guard who might come upon them at any second.

"Hey, lady," said Rutger, approaching her, "did you see who took my motorcycle?"

"Keep back!" warned Amanda.

"She has a gun, you stupid boy," snarled the guard.

"She—"

The plane's engine coughed and began to rumble. Amanda backed up carefully. As soon as she was beneath the wing, the engine was roaring. The propeller's wind whipped her coat around her ankles. Her head touched the strut, and the plane's door opened. Martha shouted, "Get in!"

Amanda threw the gun as far as she could into the darkness and scrambled up into the plane, pulling the door shut.

Curley glanced at her, and grinned. "My little gun moll," he said, flipping a switch on the panel and squinting into the darkness. "Come on, moon! Come out and give us a little light."

The baby's wails combined with the engine's roar, pounded into Amanda's head. They couldn't take off into the dreadful darkness outside.

Curley inched the plane forward slowly, then stopped, shaking his head. "We need more light!" The engine throbbed idly.

"God, help us!" cried Aunt Esther.

Suddenly Amanda's door was flung open, and the guard's hand reached for her. "No!" She screamed, kicking at him. He grabbed her ankle. She felt herself being pulled down.

Her terror turning to fury, she beat her fists on his head, but he held on.

Slowly, the moon slipped out from behind the cloud, and the plane edged forward. Amanda clutched her seat with all her strength. Curley wagged the plane slightly, sending the guard off balance for a second, long enough for Amanda to kick his shoulder and send him sprawling. She slammed the door shut, and the plane rumbled and bounced between the trees.

Suddenly they were aloft. Amanda closed her eyes and concentrated on calming her racing heartbeat. She was shaking like a twig in a windstorm and her ankle hurt.

Curley squeezed her hand. "You can open your eyes now."

She did so. He had a pleased, contented look on his face. One curly lock separated itself from the others. She longed to smooth it down but held her hand nervously in her lap.

She turned to check the group behind her. Aunt Esther lay against Uncle Jacob, her eyes squeezed tightly shut. Nathan looked out the window, while Tamara soothed the baby, whose wails had turned to a mewling cry. Martha's eyes glittered with excitement. "We made it!"

Uncle Jacob's face glowed as he said loud enough for them all to hear, *"Baruch atoh adnoy, elohaynu melech ho-lom shee-osoh li nays bamokm hazeh.* You are blessed, Lord our God, King of the Universe, Who performed a miracle for me in this place."

They were all quiet for a moment, their faces registering the awesome realization that God had indeed just performed a miracle for them.

"Amen," said Curley.

"I hope the others escaped, too," said Nathan.

"They were all gone by the time I got to the scene," said Curley, loud enough for them to hear over the engine's rumble. "So were the packages of bread."

"Where are we going?" asked Uncle Jacob.

"You're going to England," replied Curley, looking back at his passengers.

Nathan nodded and went back to his window view.

"Speaking of bread," said Martha, "have some." She opened the sack and handed out bread sticks. "How did you find us?" she asked.

Amanda and Curley related their stories, marveling at how the rescue had happened, as if guided by an unseen hand.

"I prayed we'd get out of there somehow," said Martha, a look of wonder on her face. They talked for a while longer, until Martha sighed, and relaxed in her seat, closing her eyes.

Amanda looked out at the silver-crested clouds. The vista ahead was majestic. Chewing on the crusty bread, she could think of no appropriate headline to describe it. Poetry seemed more appropriate. "It's beautiful up here!"

Curley seemed pleased that she thought so. "Look down," he said, pointing to a space between the clouds. "We're over Holland." A pleased smile curved his mouth.

As she looked down at the colorful toy-sized roofs below, Amanda wondered if he was aware of how appealing his smile was. She sighed and stretched her back. "Rutger certainly had that guard flustered."

"Rutger!" Curley glanced sideways in surprise. "I told him to keep out of it."

"He must have been watching, because he came to help me," she said. "Actually, he made himself seem like a bumbling, innocent kid only looking for his motorcycle."

"Tell me what he said and did."

When Amanda finished telling Curley exactly what happened his expression grew still. "Hmm," he said. "He may have saved his grandparents from a lot of suspicion. Even though the plane was far from their home, there is still a chance they'll be suspect. We owe him for defusing a potential bombshell."

"I wonder what will happen to the Jews." Amanda rubbed her sore ankle, thinking of the disturbing newspaper and magazine articles she'd read in the Eisenburg school library.

Curley looked grave. "We can only pray that somehow God's presence will be with them." He shook his head. "Now, you should get some rest. We'll be in England in a couple of hours."

seventeen

Curley flew them into the night, toward the moon that was setting below the clouds. He shuddered. Being trapped beneath the earth like his father was his most hideous nightmare. Shrugging off the feeling, he gazed out over the miles and miles of freedom before him. For him freedom was soaring anywhere he pleased. Why had he returned? What drew him back? He shook his head, knowing the truth. It had to be God.

Amanda's eyes were closed, her long dark lashes lying on her cheeks. Shifting moonlight and shadows played on her lovely face. Her hands lay open in her lap, giving her a vulnerable appearance. Gently reaching out, he brushed a soft wisp of hair that strayed toward him.

Every moment he spent with her made him want her more, and he wasn't used to that. It usually happened the other way: women wanted him. Unlike the others, though, Amanda hadn't pursued him. She'd simply been herself, and that was enough.

When did he start caring? It hadn't come all at once, like a bolt from the blue. That sense of familiarity he'd felt from the first moment he'd seen her. . .a memory of a long-ago air show, her eyes looking up at him, burst full-blown into his mind, and at last he remembered where and when he'd seen her before. He nearly laughed aloud, for he realized his feelings had had a logical progression after all. The seed had been planted at the air show years ago, lying dormant until her eyes caught his across the ship deck. Then it was nurtured with his admiration for her zeal-like dedication to her work, and it had blossomed when he recognized the sweetness and purity radiating from within her. He loved her courage to meet her cousin in the park; he loved her loyalty when she marched beside her family through the town. He loved her tears welling in her eyes at the plight of Hitler's innocent victims.

She had broken through his barrier against commitment. He ran a hand through his hair and frowned. Somehow she'd made him want her, and her alone. All he could see was Amanda's face.

What would happen after they landed? He couldn't imagine her married to Delbert. It was wrong. Maybe it wasn't true. He'd ask her soon.

If it were true, he'd have to get over her. He'd miss her smiles, her bright eyes as the idea for the "big story" illuminated her imagination. The idea of getting over a girl was another new experience. He'd blithely gone through adolescence and adulthood enjoying the company of women, their adoration and devotion, but moving on when one began to stir his fancy. After all, like the planes he flew, he was not made to be tied down, but like an eagle, to freely soar.

Even an eagle has a nest. The thought zinged through his brain. *Where did that come from?* he wondered. *Behold, I make all things new.*

Curley knew that voice. He glanced at Amanda again. He wanted to hold and protect her. *Lord, she may be promised to someone else. Are You telling me this feeling I have for her is just to teach me what it's going to be like when I find the right woman?* Or was this retribution? Letting him know how it felt to be unlucky in love?

Love? Where did that word come from? But the idea of loving someone other than Amanda was suddenly distasteful.

He pulled out his clipboard, looked at the lights below, and studied the map. To keep his errant thoughts from straying back to Amanda, he concentrated on the terrain and the list of German airfields and number of planes he'd observed. Something was up. Who would be the target of all those planes Hitler was gathering?

❧

Amanda awoke, realizing the sound of the engine had changed

and they were descending. She hunched her shoulders and stretched her arms straight over her lap, then raked her hair back into place.

Curley lifted one eyebrow and grinned at her. "Feel better?"

"Yes. How long did I sleep?"

"About two hours. We're over the east English coast.

The first piercing rays of dawn touched the tips of trees and houses below, turning them to liquid gold. A vast amount of water on her side was changing from gray to blue even as she watched.

"They call that The Wash," said Curley, leaning over her and looking down into the bay. He banked the plane to the left, glancing at the land below and back to the map.

Amanda looked back at her family with compassion. Martha lay scrunched up around the armrests on two seats, Aunt Esther still lay against Uncle Jacob, his jacket over her, and he leaned against the wall. Nathan sprawled straight in his seat, legs thrust beneath Martha's seat, head back, sound asleep. Tamara had just finished diapering the baby on her lap. She gave Amanda a sad smile and pulled the baby's bunting down over his feet.

Amanda smiled back, then turned to look ahead. Rosy-hued, gold-tipped spires stood like sentinels among lower-roofed building. They loomed closer as the plane dipped lower.

By the time the wheels touched the ground, the passengers were awake. Aunt Esther straightened her clothes, Uncle Jacob pulled the sleeves of his jacket down over his wrists, Martha ran a comb through her pale hair. Nathan bent forward, tying his shoes, while Tamara held the baby to her shoulder, gently patting his back.

Four jeeps drew close the minute Curley cut the engine. "Wait here," he said and climbed out. He saluted to the approaching officer. "Captain Cameron reporting, sir. I wasn't able to complete my mission. Civilians are on board in need of assistance."

The officer looked up at faces crowded in the plane's window. "Explain."

Later, as the family sipped coffee in the barracks, Amanda cabled her parents, then she and Curley slipped outside. He tucked her hand in the crook of his elbow and they walked in the nippy morning air. Small bushes swept down the hillsides, blanketing the landscape in autumn gold and green.

"I have to leave soon," he said. The thought of her marrying Delbert haunted him. He raked his fingers through his hair. How could he ask her about it without seeming nosey or jealous?

"Where are you going?" she asked.

"Back to the States to report to my commanding officer. I was supposed to take the Vega to Holland. But my orders have been changed."

"We'll always be grateful to you," she said.

The heartrending tenderness in her gaze drew a wave of love over his heart. Confused, he shrugged. "I was glad I was there for you." They found a gate, and he pushed it open.

"Don't be modest. You're a knight in shining armor." They strolled along a path, between a line of elms, stopping at an arbor. Amanda sat on the stone bench, and Curley stood facing her with one foot on the bench beside her, bracing his right forearm on his thigh. "We have to talk," he said impatiently. "I heard you'll be marrying Delbert when you get back and—"

"Delbert?" Amanda's nose wrinkled. "I'm not marrying him!"

"But he said—"

"I don't care what he said." Amanda stood, and poked Curley's chest. His foot came down, and he leaned back slightly. "Men! I'm so sick of men deciding where I'll be going, with whom, when, and how! And Delbert can go jump in a lake."

"Hold on! You're not classifying me in with the rest of those men, are you?" He gripped both of her shoulders. "I'm not trying to talk you into doing anything. I want a companion, an equal, not a slave." He hesitated, then added, "That is, if I ever decide to. . ." He dropped his hands from her shoulders, disgusted at himself for sounding like a bumbling adolescent.

"Curley?" Hearing his name on her lips almost stole his breath away.

Amanda reached up and put her hand on his cheek. Dark green specks glowed in the artless gaze she fixed on him. "If you ever want a companion, a friend, I'll be there."

That promise filled him with intense happiness. All his excuses to keep from getting tied down by some wily female were going down in flames. The cynical reckless bachelor, the lone eagle persona, suddenly no longer suited him. He had thought falling in love was being caught in a trap, but it wasn't like that at all. Instead, he felt a soaring freedom, as if a dozen invisible restraints had just been broken.

For a long moment they simply stood there, looking at each other. *She's not marrying Delbert!* A breeze moved through the trees, a finch whistled a lilting tune, and his heart sang along. She seemed to be waiting for him to say something.

"Marry me, Amanda." Another finch answered the first one.

She stared at him, her green eyes misting. Romantic cliches sprang to mind. She took a shaky breath. "This is rather sudden, don't you think?"

"No. On the plane I suddenly remembered seeing you years ago at an air show. I knew then there was something special about you. Then from the moment I landed on that ship and took another look, I knew I loved you."

"You what?"

He looked down at her for a second, then groaned and hugged her to him. "I love you, Amanda. I didn't realize it until I almost lost you to those Germans. Or to Delbert."

"Oh, Curley," she sighed. "You were right. If I'd listened to you I wouldn't have been captured." Then she lifted her chin. "But we wouldn't have rescued my family either. I would never have known what had happened to them if I hadn't been captured along with them."

He cupped her face in his hands, marveling at the petal softness of her skin. "God and I will always take care of you. Can you believe that?"

Amanda nodded, brushing a tear from her eye. Ever since she met him at that air show, she'd wanted him. This was one request she hadn't dared make to God, but He'd known. "I love you, too," she said. "I've loved you since I was seventeen years old."

Suddenly Curley dropped to one knee, took her hand, and brought it to his chest. She felt his warmth beneath his jacket. He looked up at her with a mixture of boyish exuberance and earnestness that made her knees weak.

"Amanda Chase, will you marry me?"

She smiled down into his eyes, blissful happiness flowing over her like a warm wave.

Before she could answer, he went on, "First, there's something you must know: I don't want you to stop doing what you love. Chasing down stories and reporting is in your blood, and it's one of your lovable charms. Of course, if you want to quit and settle down—"

"Yes."

"Yes?"

"Yes, James Cameron. I'll marry you." He rose in one fluid motion. She flung her arms around him, burying her face in his shoulder.

He talked about his duty to the Army, she of her excitement for writing the truth about what was happening in Germany. He told her of the air race of the century starting that week, in Middlesex, with aces in their souped-up planes racing for Australia. "I'll pull some strings and get you a special press pass. Watch the Comet," he said. "It's the fastest thing with wings—next to my little Moth," he added, grinning modestly.

They made plans to meet and announce their engagement as soon as she arrived back in the States. Amanda felt peace, like a comforting aroma, enveloping them. She sighed. "This is a fairy tale and I'm the girl who got the prince."

He laughed and pulled her away with him. "Come on, princess. Let's go live happily ever after!"

epilogue

Jerusalem, 1977

"God delivered Cousin Joseph's grandparents, but others were not so fortunate," said Curley to his youngest grandson, Sam. They were leaving the Yad Vashem, memorial of the holocaust.

"Were you there?" Sam spoke softly, matching their respectful mood.

"We almost were," said Amanda, putting a hand on his slender shoulder. "But your grandpa rescued us in his airplane."

The boy looked up at them, excitement shining in his eyes. "Did you shoot 'em out of the sky?"

"No, Grandma knocked him flat on his back before we even took off." Curley caught Amanda's eye and winked.

"Wow! How did you do that, Grandma?"

"Hold still," said Amanda, removing the temporary *yarmulke* he had to wear to enter the memorial. Sunshine glinted off his curly auburn hair. "I'll tell you all about it this afternoon when we get back to Cousin Martha's house."

Sam walked ahead of them, shuffling through the postcards they'd bought. Amanda shuddered, and Curley hugged her to his side. "Are you okay?"

"Yes." She looked back at the monument. "When I think that Uncle Jacob almost went back—"

He stopped and put both hands on her waist. Their eyes on each other, he said, "Think back. No one in 1934 could have seen the horror that was coming. Many thought it was temporary and they'd get their homes and lives back. I know you feel sad; so do I, but we both had the satisfaction of helping put a stop to that madman. You with your words, and me with the air corps."

She glanced back at the building again. "But so many!

Millions, each one with hopes, dreams, memories, a different story for each life."

Sam tugged at her sleeve. "Please, can I have my candy now, Grandma?"

Amanda took the postcards, put them into her purse, and drew out a candy bar. Sam walked beside them, tearing the paper off.

Hand in hand they walked down the sidewalk to their car. "I can hardly bare to think of the Holocaust," said Amanda. "Thank God for this memorial."

Curley squeezed her hand. "God willing, the world won't forget—so that it will never happen again."

A Letter To Our Readers

Dear Reader:

In order that we might better contribute to your reading enjoyment, we would appreciate your taking a few minutes to respond to the following questions. When completed, please return to the following:

Rebecca Germany, Managing Editor
Heartsong Presents
P.O. Box 719
Uhrichsville, Ohio 44683

1. Did you enjoy reading *Escape on the Wind*?
   ❑ Very much. I would like to see more books
      by this author!
   ❑ Moderately
      I would have enjoyed it more if _____

      _____

2. Are you a member of **Heartsong Presents**? ❑Yes ❑No
   If no, where did you purchase this book?_____

   _____

3. What influenced your decision to purchase this
   book? (Check those that apply.)

   ❑ Cover   ❑ Back cover copy

   ❑ Title   ❑ Friends

   ❑ Publicity   ❑ Other_____

4. How would you rate, on a scale from 1 (poor) to 5
   (superior), the cover design?_____

5. On a scale from 1 (poor) to 10 (superior), please rate the following elements.

  ___Heroine   ___Plot

  ___Hero   ___Inspirational theme

  ___Setting   ___Secondary characters

6. What settings would you like to see covered in **Heartsong Presents** books?_____

   _____

   _____

7. What are some inspirational themes you would like to see treated in future books?_____

   _____

   _____

8. Would you be interested in reading other **Heartsong Presents** titles?   ❑ Yes   ❑ No

9. Please check your age range:
   ❑ Under 18   ❑ 18-24   ❑ 25-34
   ❑ 35-45   ❑ 46-55   ❑ Over 55

10. How many hours per week do you read? _____

Name _____

Occupation_____

Address_____

City_____ State_____ Zip _____

·····Hearts♥ng ·····

Any 12 *Heartsong* Presents titles for only $26.95 *

*plus $1.00 shipping and handling per order and sales tax where applicable.

HISTORICAL ROMANCE IS CHEAPER BY THE DOZEN! Buy any assortment of twelve *Heartsong Presents* titles and save 25% off of the already discounted price of $2.95 each!

HEARTSONG PRESENTS TITLES AVAILABLE NOW:

__HP 64 CROWS'-NESTS AND MIRRORS, *Colleen L. Reece*

__HP103 LOVE'S SHINING HOPE, *JoAnn A. Grote*

__HP111 A KINGDOM DIVIDED, *Tracie J. Peterson*

__HP112 CAPTIVES OF THE CANYON, *Colleen L. Reece*

__HP127 FOREVER YOURS, *Tracie J. Peterson*

__HP131 LOVE IN THE PRAIRIE WILDS, *Robin Chandler*

__HP132 LOST CREEK MISSION, *Cheryl Tenbrook*

__HP135 SIGN OF THE SPIRIT, *Kay Cornelius*

__HP140 ANGEL'S CAUSE, *Tracie J. Peterson*

__HP143 MORNING MOUNTAIN, *Peggy Darty*

__HP144 FLOWER OF THE WEST, *Colleen L. Reece*

__HP163 DREAMS OF GLORY, *Linda Herring*

__HP164 ALAS MY LOVE, *Tracie J. Peterson*

__HP167 PRISCILLA HIRES A HUSBAND, *Loree Lough*

__HP168 LOVE SHALL COME AGAIN, *Birdie L. Etchison*

__HP175 JAMES'S JOY, *Cara McCormack*

__HP176 WHERE THERE IS HOPE, *Carolyn R. Scheidies*

__HP179 HER FATHER'S LOVE, *Nancy Lavo*

__HP180 FRIEND OF A FRIEND, *Jill Richardson*

__HP183 A NEW LOVE, *VeraLee Wiggins*

__HP184 THE HOPE THAT SINGS, *JoAnn A. Grote*

__HP187 FLOWER OF ALASKA, *Colleen L. Reece*

__HP188 AN UNCERTAIN HEART, *Andrea Boeshaar*

__HP191 SMALL BLESSINGS, *DeWanna Pace*

__HP192 FROM ASHES TO GLORY, *Bonnie L. Crank*

__HP195 COME AWAY MY LOVE, *Tracie J. Peterson*

__HP196 DREAMS FULFILLED, *Linda Herring*

__HP199 DAKOTA DECEMBER, *Lauraine Snelling*

__HP200 IF ONLY, *Tracie J. Peterson*

__HP203 AMPLE PORTIONS, *Dianne L. Christner*

__HP204 MEGAN'S CHOICE, *Rosey Dow*

__HP207 THE EAGLE AND THE LAMB, *Darlene Mindrup*

(If ordering from this page, please remember to include it with the order form.)

·········· Presents ··········

__HP208 LOVE'S TENDER PATH, *Birdie L.*
　　　　Etchison
__HP211 MY VALENTINE, *Tracie J.*
　　　　Peterson
__HP215 TULSA TRESPASS, *Norma Jean Lutz*
__HP216 BLACK HAWK'S FEATHER,
　　　　Carolyn R. Scheidies
__HP219 A HEART FOR HOME, *Norene*
　　　　Morris
__HP220 SONG OF THE DOVE, *Peggy Darty*
__HP223 THREADS OF LOVE, *Judith*
　　　　McCoy Miller
__HP224 EDGE OF DESTINY, *Darlene*
　　　　Mindrup
__HP227 BRIDGET'S BARGAIN, *Loree Lough*

__HP228 FALLING WATER VALLEY, *Mary*
　　　　Louise Colln
__HP235 THE LADY ROSE, *Joyce Williams*
__HP236 VALIANT HEART, *Sally Laity*
__HP239 LOGAN'S LADY, *Tracie J. Peterson*
__HP240 THE SUN STILL SHINES, *Linda Ford*
__HP243 THE RISING SUN, *Darlene Mindrup*
__HP244 WOVEN THREADS, *Judith McCoy*
　　　　Miller
__HP247 STRONG AS THE REDWOOD,
　　　　Kristin Billerbeck
__HP248 RETURN TO TULSA, *Norma Jean*
　　　　Lutz
__HP251 ESCAPE ON THE WIND, *Jane*
　　　　LaMunyon
__HP252 ANNA'S HOPE, *Birdie L. Etchison*

Great Inspirational Romance at a Great Price!

Heartsong Presents books are inspirational romances in contemporary and historical settings, designed to give you an enjoyable, spirit-lifting reading experience. You can choose wonderfully written titles from some of today's best authors like Peggy Darty, Sally Laity, Tracie Peterson, Colleen L. Reece, Lauraine Snelling, and many others.

When ordering quantities less than twelve, above titles are $2.95 each.
Not all titles may be available at time of order.

Hearts♥ng Presents
Love Stories Are Rated G!

That's for godly, gratifying, and of course, great! If you love a thrilling love story, but don't appreciate the sordidness of some popular paperback romances, **Heartsong Presents** is for you. In fact, **Heartsong Presents** is the *only inspirational romance book club*, the only one featuring love stories where Christian faith is the primary ingredient in a marriage relationship.

Sign up today to receive your first set of four, never before published Christian romances. Send no money now; you will receive a bill with the first shipment. You may cancel at any time without obligation, and if you aren't completely satisfied with any selection, you may return the books for an immediate refund!

Imagine. . .four new romances every four weeks—two historical, two contemporary—with men and women like you who long to meet the one God has chosen as the love of their lives. . .all for the low price of $9.97 postpaid.

To join, simply complete the coupon below and mail to the address provided. **Heartsong Presents** romances are rated G for another reason: They'll arrive *Godspeed!*